“Can you guarantee the safe return of my son?”

Yes, Spencer had spent a decade in covert operations and a good deal of that time in the Middle East. Not a problem. But this wasn’t as cut-and-dried as a military operation. This was a small boy, whose life and future hung in the balance.

Willow Harris stared at him expectantly. He understood what she was looking for.

“I can tell you that I have a perfect record, no failures whatsoever.”

Willow’s expression brightened as she let out an audible sigh. “Good. When do we leave?”

“We?”

Her gaze locked with his. He didn’t miss the determination there or the underlying fear.

“If I have to make a choice between saving you or saving the child, I will save the child.” He allowed the ramifications of those words to sink in a second or two before he continued. “Are you prepared for that?”

Three, four, then five beats passed.

“Yes.”

So much for the scare tactics. “In that case,” he relented, “we’ll begin preparations tomorrow.”

DEBRA WEBB

A SOLDIER'S OATH

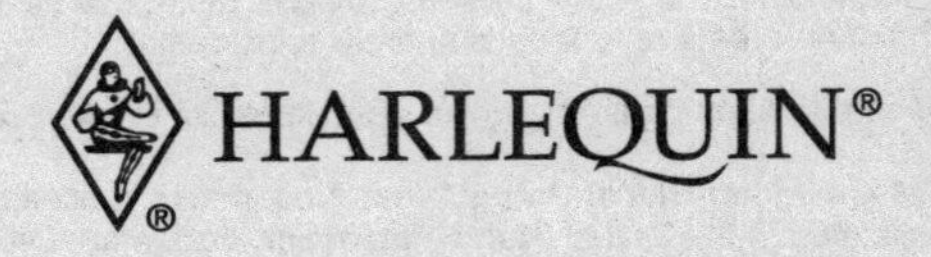

TORONTO • NEW YORK • LONDON
AMSTERDAM • PARIS • SYDNEY • HAMBURG
STOCKHOLM • ATHENS • TOKYO • MILAN • MADRID
PRAGUE • WARSAW • BUDAPEST • AUCKLAND

This book is dedicated to all the fans of the Colby Agency. Thank you for your faithfulness to this series. Please enjoy the first in this new trilogy revolving around Jim Colby, Victoria's son.

ISBN-13: 978-0-373-69250-7
ISBN-10: 0-373-69250-1

A SOLDIER'S OATH

This edition published by arrangement with Harlequin Books S.A.

www.eHarlequin.com

Printed in U.S.A.

ABOUT THE AUTHOR

Debra Webb was born in Scottsboro, Alabama, to parents who taught her that anything is possible if you want it bad enough. She began writing at age nine. Eventually, she met and married the man of her dreams, and then tried various occupations, including selling vacuum cleaners, working in a factory, a daycare center, a hospital and a department store. When her husband joined the military, they moved to Berlin, Germany, and Debra became a secretary in the commanding general's office. By 1985 they were back in the States, and finally moved to Tennessee, to a small town where everyone knows everyone else. With the support of her husband and two beautiful daughters, Debra took up writing again, looking to mystery and movies for inspiration. In 1998, her dream of writing for Harlequin Books came true. You can write to Debra at P.O. Box 64, Huntland, Tennessee 37345 or visit her Web site at www.debrawebb.com to find out exciting news about her next book.

Books by Debra Webb

HARLEQUIN INTRIGUE

837—JOHN DOE ON HER DOORSTEP*
843—EXECUTIVE BODYGUARD*
849—MAN OF HER DREAMS*
864—URBAN SENSATION
891—PERSON OF INTEREST
909—INVESTIGATING 101**
916—RAW TALENT**
934—THE HIDDEN HEIR**
951—A COLBY CHRISTMAS**
983—A SOLDIER'S OATH†

*The Enforcers
**Colby Agency
†The Equalizers

CAST OF CHARACTERS

Jim Colby—The head of the Equalizers and the son of Victoria Colby-Camp. Jim needs a fresh start.

Victoria Colby-Camp—The head of the Colby Agency. Victoria wants the best for her son, even if it means he doesn't come to work for her at the Colby Agency.

Tasha Colby—Jim's wife and the mother of their daughter, Jamie.

Willow Harris—Willow will do anything to get her son Ata back from his manipulative and treacherous father who lives in Kuwait.

Spencer Anders—Former Special Forces major, Anders knows the Middle East like the back of his hand. He just hadn't anticipated a covert op to the Middle East with an untrained female civilian in tow.

Khaled al-Shimmari—Khaled will kill anyone who goes near his son, his only heir. Proving his ties to terrorists won't be easy, but may very well be deadly.

Connie Gardner—The new receptionist for the Equalizers.

Renee Vaughn—A former prosecutor. She is ready to stop playing it so straight and safe and start infusing some danger into her life. Maybe the Equalizers is the place to start.

Sam Johnson—The grittiest new associate at the Equalizers. Don't mess with Sam or you might just wind up dead.

Chapter One

Friday, February 18
St. Louis, Missouri

Willow Harris shifted the car into Park and turned off the engine. She drew in a slow, deep breath and ordered herself to remain calm.

This particular part of the east side of St. Louis wasn't exactly the kind of place a woman wanted to find herself in at dusk, but she had no choice.

He'd called.

She'd had to come, no matter the time of day or night. The man she'd driven here to see didn't keep the usual business hours.

Before getting out of the car she said one last prayer. *Please, God, let the news be good.* She wasn't sure she could take any more bad news.

Eight months.

She'd been fighting to get her son back for eight long months. An eternity. Hurt welled up inside her at the idea that she'd missed his second birthday. Just last week. She'd missed so much already. All those evolving toddler moments. Precious changes that no mother should miss.

Nothing would bring those moments back.

Closing her eyes, she forced the painful thoughts away. She had to be strong. She would never be able to bring her baby home again if she couldn't hold herself together better than this.

"Whatever it takes," she murmured as she opened her eyes and firmed her resolve. No weakness, no fear. "I will do *whatever it takes*."

Willow emerged from her car and headed for the office of Davenport Investigations. She'd been here several times before. But this time was different. This time she would be given an update on the man who'd actually managed to get close enough to send back pictures of her son.

No one had gotten that close before.

Anticipation fluttered in her chest.

She couldn't wait to see the pictures of her baby.

Eight endless months had passed since she'd last seen him.

She hadn't been able to hold him…to kiss his sweet little head. Maybe if she were really lucky, this man would be able to reunite her with her precious child.

After numerous failures he could be the one.

The bell over the door jingled as she entered the

suite of offices that sat tucked between a dry cleaning service and a small chain drug store, both of which had long ago gone out of business. The small waiting room was empty and absolutely silent as usual. Not once during her four previous visits had she encountered another client. Mr. Davenport explained that he carefully arranged appointments to ensure complete privacy. As much as she understood that need, walking into his office alone this close to dark made her a little uneasy.

Whatever it takes, she reminded herself.

She passed two upholstered chairs flanking an end table, the magazine-cluttered top highlighted by the dim glow showering down from a ceramic lamp. No desk, no chair, no telephone and, evidently, no receptionist. Just a space-challenged room designed for waiting.

Since she'd timed her arrival to the minute—experience had taught her not to bother coming early—she strode up to the door that led into Davenport's private office and knocked. He should be waiting for her to show up about now.

"Come in, Ms. Harris," he called through the closed door.

Willow moistened her lips, took another deep breath and entered his office.

He sat behind his massive wooden desk, didn't bother standing as he gestured for her to have a seat. She'd wondered at his lack of social etiquette at first, but the hope that he could help her had overridden any second thoughts. Desperation had a way of doing that.

His desk, credenza and file cabinets were clear of clutter as if he'd taken care to lock away every single scrap of paper that might reveal information regarding one of his clients. However lacking in decorum he might be, he was definitely discreet.

"You have good news?" she asked as she settled into the lone chair on her side of his desk. "And the pictures?" Hope bloomed in her chest at the mere idea of seeing her baby, even if only in covertly snapped photos.

He tossed an envelope in her direction. "I received these day before yesterday."

Willow didn't ask why he hadn't let her know about the pictures before today. Nor did she inquire as to why he avoided giving her an answer as to whether or not he had good news. He most likely had his reasons for doling out information in the way he did, reasons she probably wouldn't want to know. That was something else she'd learned about this man, he didn't like prying questions unless he was the one doing the asking. Her fingers trembled as she opened the envelope and took out the digital prints. Her heart thumped hard and tears burned in her eyes.

Ata.

Her baby.

He looked so big…so different. Two years old. And

she'd missed that special day. The need to hold him was suddenly so intense that she could scarcely breathe.

How could the man she'd thought she loved, the man she'd trusted and married, have done this to her? Somewhere in the back of her mind a voice taunted her, reminding her that she should have listened to her parents. They would tell her that this was the price she paid for getting in bed with the devil. Her stomach knotted violently and she pushed the painful thoughts away.

Yes, she'd made a mistake. But surely God would not consider taking her child from her reasonable punishment for an innocent error in judgment. She refused to believe as her parents did. If that made her evil, then so be it.

Clearing her mind of the ugly past that represented her dysfunctional childhood, she shuffled through picture after picture, her heart bursting with equal measures of joy and sadness. Ata playing on the balcony outside her former husband's home. Her baby's face pressed against the glass of a car window. Him toddling around her ex-husband's mother in the market.

Davenport's man had gotten very close.

Close enough to reach out and touch her baby.

She held the pictures against her chest and lifted her gaze to the waiting investigator. "How soon does he think he can make a move?"

This was the moment she had waited for—prayed for—night after night for so very long.

"We have a problem, Ms. Harris."

Her heart dropped, landing somewhere in the vicinity of her stomach.

Raymond Davenport was not a man she could even hope to read or assess in any way. His expression remained as impassive, as utterly devoid of emotion as a lamp post. But something in his tone, the subtlest note of defeat or disappointment had dread crushing against her vital organs and seeping deep into her bones.

"I don't understand." There couldn't be a problem. Not now. They were so close. "You said your man had gotten close to my son." She held out the pictures. "The proof is right here. What could go wrong?"

"We've had no further contact since I received the photos."

Fear, stark and brutal, roared through her, ruptured the thin membrane of hope. She instinctively knew that this was very bad news.

"On an extremely sensitive job like this one," Davenport went on, "when you lose contact for more than twenty-four hours that usually means only one thing...*trouble*."

She didn't want to hear this. Dear God, she did not want to hear this. It couldn't be true...*please don't let it be true.*

Davenport leaned forward, propped his hands on his desk. The hard-earned experience and cool distance usually in his eyes were overshadowed by something softer, something very much like sympathy. “Ms. Harris, I understand how badly you want to get your boy back. Believe me. I have two sons of my own and grandkids. Every day you have to wait is pure hell, but…”

She wanted to speak up…to tell him not to say more. She didn’t want to hear what she knew was coming. But she couldn’t force the words from her lips.

“…yours is not the first case like this I’ve worked. The culture we’re dealing with in this situation is completely different. Winning by legal means is impossible, you’ve learned that the hard way. Stealing the child back is usually the only option for a parent faced with these circumstances.”

He paused, and in that moment Willow recognized with slowly building horror that, in this man’s opinion, all hope was lost…again.

Before she could protest his unspoken assessment, he continued, “That said, your position is different in yet another way. Your ex-husband and his family are…unique.”

In this instance *unique* was just another word for untouchable. The al-Shimmari family was *connected,* socially and politically. Immense wealth added to their power. The Kuwaiti authorities wouldn’t dare cross the family.

“Are you saying I should give up hope?” She wouldn’t. Never. Never. She would keep looking until she found someone who could help her. If not this man, then someone else. Nothing he could say would change her mind.

"I'm saying, Ms. Harris," he offered quietly, far too quietly for such a brusque man, "that you're looking for a miracle and you're not going to find it. Your ex-husband will order the execution of anyone who gets close to the child. If my man is dead—and I suspect he is—then *no one* is going to be able to get close enough to get your son back."

With a strength she couldn't fathom the source of, Willow restrained the tears that threatened. "Thank you, Mr. Davenport." She stood. "I assume the pictures are mine to keep." How she said this without her voice wobbling she couldn't imagine.

He nodded. "Of course."

She squared her shoulders in an effort to hold onto her disintegrating composure a moment longer. "You'll send me a final bill?"

"Let's call it even, Ms. Harris." He pushed out of his chair and stood, another first in her presence. "You take care of yourself now."

Somehow she pivoted on her heel and walked out of his office. She didn't recall crossing the sidewalk or even getting into her car. Awareness of time and place didn't connect again until she was driving away, the pictures of her son spread across the passenger seat.

Choosing Davenport had obviously been a mistake. She tightened her grip on the steering wheel.

Of course it had been. If he'd lived up to his renowned reputation, she would not be leaving empty-handed. This was nothing more than a minor setback. She would find a new private investigator. A better one. Someone who could get the job done without any excuses. She would start her search for someone more qualified right now. This minute.

...you're looking for a miracle and you're not going to find it.

She blinked back the emotion brimming on her lashes. No. Dammit. He was wrong. She was not looking for a miracle. She didn't need a miracle. All she needed was a man cunning enough and fearless enough to get the job done.

Chicago, Illinois
Same Day

JAMES COLBY, Jr., Jim to the handful of people close to him, waited several minutes before he entered the bar.

It had been a long time since he'd gone into an establishment like this. Maybe not long enough, he mused as he took a long look around. Places like this represented his old life...a life that, thankfully, no longer existed.

The room was dimly lit, the cigarette smoke thick in the air despite the current regulations on smoking in public places. A scattering of tables stood between him and the bar that snaked its way around the length and width of two walls. Few of the stools were occupied and even fewer of the tables. Then again, at 6:15 p.m. it was still fairly early. The crowd, if there was to be one, likely crawled out of the woodwork later in the night.

But Jim wasn't looking for a crowd. Actually, the fewer patrons the better for his purposes. He seriously doubted that the man he'd come to see would hang around once the place got busy. All the more reason to stop wasting time and to get this done.

Spencer Anders sat on the stool farthest from the entrance, his back to the wall. He'd watched Jim enter the bar. He watched now as he approached.

Some three yards from his position was an emergency exit. Jim supposed Anders could use that egress for a hasty retreat if he wasn't in the mood for company. But he didn't. He sat there and continued to observe the man closing in on his position.

Jim strode across the room and took a seat a couple of stools this side of the other man. No need to crowd him.

"Spencer Anders?"

Anders downed the last swallow of his bourbon. "That's right."

"My name is Jim Colby. I have a proposition for you."

"Well, Jim Colby—" Anders placed his empty glass on the bar "—you've been misinformed as to my status." He stood and tossed a couple of bills on the bar to cover his tab. "I'm not looking for any propositions."

Jim kept his smile to himself. He didn't want to tick the guy off, but neither did he want to let him get away. "I heard you were looking for steady employment."

"Really? Who're you?" Anders challenged, "an employment service representative?"

Chicago's population amounted to about four million people. Finding one former army major who didn't want to be found would have taken some time and initiative under normal circumstances. Since tracking Anders to this place, his regular hangout since arriving in Chicago three months prior, hadn't been that difficult, Jim had to assume he wanted to be found despite his get-lost attitude. Anders had taken a room in a nearby motel that served more as a halfway house than anything one might find in a travel guide. He accepted temporary jobs that required only hard labor and no real sense of purpose. He never stayed on long enough to make friends. So far as Jim could see, he spent most of his time making enemies.

"A mutual friend mentioned you were in town seeking a new career direction."

This got ex-Major Anders's attention. For the past two years his MO appeared to include moving on once he'd worn out his welcome. Whether he actually tried to pull his life together after settling in each new location was unknown, but the end result was always the same.

"You must have me confused with someone else, Mr. Colby." He allowed his gaze to zero in fully on Jim's so that there was no misunderstanding as to the finality of his words. "I don't have any friends."

Spencer Anders would have walked away then and there with no further discussion, Jim decided, if he hadn't played the ace up his sleeve.

"Lucas Camp tells me you're the best in covert and low-visibility operations."

Anders hesitated. For three beats Jim wasn't sure if he would turn around or if he would just walk on out. But then he executed an about-face and moved back to the stool he'd vacated.

When Anders's gaze rested on Jim's once more, he said, "I've never worked directly for or with Mr. Camp. I'm surprised he even knows my name. The way I heard it he's retired now."

That was true.

"What's your connection to him?" Anders wanted to know.

Jim had expected that one.

"He married Victoria Colby, my mother."

Anders's eyes narrowed, but not with suspicion. "You're from the Colby Agency?" The name appeared to connect fully for him then.

Jim wasn't surprised that the man recognized his mother's name or that of her agency. The Colby Agency was one of the top private investigations agencies in the country. A man with a background like Anders would consider P.I. firms when searching for employment. In his case, however, that same background prevented him from applying to most.

"I'm not here representing the Colby Agency."

The anticipation that had tapered Anders's focus vanished. "I'm certain you're a busy man, Mr. Colby. Why don't we cut through all the crap and get straight to the point?"

Jim liked this guy already. "I've recently opened my own firm, Mr. Anders. You have the training I'm looking for as well as extensive experience in the Middle East. Considering current events and the Middle East's ongoing status as a hot spot politically as well as economically, I need that kind of experience on my team. I have a vacancy and I'd like you to fill it."

Anders motioned for the bartender to refill his empty tumbler. "You drinking anything?" he said to Jim.

Jim shook his head. That he wasn't even momentarily tempted gave him great satisfaction. That Anders would offer suggested interest in his proposition.

The bartender sidled over and splashed a couple of fingers of bourbon into the other man's empty glass. When he'd moved out of earshot to take care of the next customer, Anders said, "Why open another P.I. firm? You have a problem working for your mother?"

Jim got those questions often, especially from the investigators at the Colby Agency. He would have been welcome there by all on staff. Victoria Colby-Camp had expected Jim to take over one day. But he had other plans. No…not plans…needs. He needed to do this. And that need had nothing to do with any inability to work with or for his mother.

"What I have in mind doesn't fit the mold, Mr. Anders. I'm afraid my mother would be startled at some of the methods I might choose to utilize."

Still visibly skeptical, Anders sipped his drink before suggesting, "Perhaps Mr. Camp didn't completely fill you in on my less-than-desirable work history."

Jim resisted the impulse to argue that if he wanted to compare histories he would gladly give him a run for his money on who had the ugliest past. But he would save that for another time.

"I'm aware of the circumstances surrounding the way you separated from military service if that's what you mean." And it was, of course. Spencer Anders had a stellar record other than that final nasty smudge. Discounting, of course, a number of misdemeanor disorderly conducts in public establishments very much like this one since leaving the military.

The suspicion Jim had expected to see earlier made its appearance at that point. He understood. Most prospective employers would be put off by the idea of a general military discharge. It wasn't quite a dishonorable discharge, but it carried an equally unattractive stigma. But Jim knew something most didn't, Spencer Anders had been railroaded by a superior officer.

The fact that his betrayal couldn't be proven beyond a shadow of a doubt was the reason he'd been charged with the lesser offences of insubordination and conduct unbecoming of an officer rather than being shipped off to spend a life sentence in a military prison. Those seemingly lesser charges had carried a stiff, humiliating penance of their own. Anders had been stripped of rank, all the way down to a first lieutenant, and then generally discharged when he opted to resign rather than accept the charges and grovel as expected.

Then again, to a man like Anders, being labeled a traitor to his country was pretty much a life sentence in itself.

"Then I have to question just what sort of firm you plan to operate, Mr. Colby."

Jim appreciated his frankness.

"Did your source also tell you," Anders went on before Jim could respond to his last statement, "about my difficulties since leaving military service?"

Spencer Anders had separated from the U.S. Army two years ago. Since then he'd spent most of his time in dives not unlike this one, attempting to obliterate the past; only the towns changed. His blood alcohol level lingered above the legal limit more often than not, Jim would wager. He also recognized the strategy. Been there, done that. But booze wasn't the answer to Anders's problems. Telling him so wouldn't help. This was something he had to come to terms with on his own.

"As long as you stay sober on the job, I don't care what you do in your free time." Jim, of all people, understood what made a man like Anders turn to the bottle for a solace found no other place. The bad habit was taken up for a single, unhealthy reason and would be dumped for the same. He wouldn't need any twelve-step program, all he needed was his self-worth back.

That would come in time given the right circumstances.

Anders finished off the bourbon. "Just because I was forced out of the army doesn't mean I'm interested in a life of anything beyond the occasional barroom brawl. Believe it or not, high crimes aren't my style."

Jim almost laughed at that. "There are times," he admitted, "when working within the law won't get the job done. But I'm not talking about breaking the law for the sake of breaking it, Mr. Anders. I'm only talking about going slightly beyond it and perhaps ignoring some aspects of it when the need arises."

"Well, good luck to you, Mr. Colby. As much as I appreciate the offer, I'm not sure I'm the man you're looking for."

Jim took a business card from his coat pocket and laid it on the bar. "Call me if you change your mind. The doors open Monday morning, and I'd like you there when that happens."

He didn't wait for a response.

As he drove away, Jim wondered how long it

would take the man to decide he needed a second chance badly enough to risk failure and betrayal.

Jim knew firsthand how hard it was to meet that particular challenge and the expectations that went along with treading out onto that shaky limb. Sometimes the fear of failure was the scariest part of all.

He thought about his wife and baby girl. There wasn't a day that passed that Jim didn't consider whether or not he could be the man, the husband and father, those two needed him to be.

Was starting his own venture part of that whole I-don't-want-to-fail scenario? With his own business he would set the rules, answering only to himself. No one else would be holding a preconceived measurement or standard of success against his every endeavor.

The thought had crossed his mind, more than once if he admitted the truth.

Just a little baggage of his own he had to carry around until he got past it.

Jim drove to the South Loop and took the exit that led to his new suite of offices. The old brownstone needed some renovation but nothing he couldn't handle in time.

After parking in the back alley, he unlocked the rear entrance and flipped on the lights. He should have gone home. Tasha would be wondering if he planned to make every night a late night. But he'd wanted to check the answering machine before going home. He'd made a few calls this afternoon, and he hoped to get some timely responses.

He made his way to the front room that was now a lobby, turning on lights as he went. When he was halfway up the stairs to the second floor the doorbell buzzed; someone was at the door.

His first thought was that Tasha had come to drag him home, but bringing Jamie out in the blustery February weather wasn't his wife's technique. She'd call and order him to get home.

Could be his first customer. He had hung up a shingle of sorts today.

Or, if he was lucky, it would be Anders to come to say he'd thought about Jim's offer and wanted the job.

A grin slid across Jim's face as he opened the door and identified his visitor. None of the above.

"Mom." He leaned against the door frame and crossed his arms over his chest. "Come to see what I've done with the place?"

Victoria Colby-Camp returned his smile. "I'm sure you haven't had time to do that much. But you'll get it done."

That she believed in him so completely no matter how many times he missed the mark or fell down as he tried to turn his life around still surprised him. She was a hell of a mom for a guy who'd gone as low as it was humanly possible to go.

He glanced past her. "Where's your other half?"

Victoria rarely went anywhere without Lucas unless he was out of town and she had no other choice. The two were inseparable.

"He's keeping your lovely wife and our granddaughter company while dinner gets cold."

Dinner. Oh, man. He'd forgotten. Dammit.

"Just let me check my voice mail and lock up and I'm on my way."

"I'll ride along with you," she offered. "Lucas can bring me by to pick up my car later."

Jim let the smile nudging at his lips do what it would. He'd never been big on smiles, but these days the women in his life knew how to draw them out of him. His mother knew him all too well. If she didn't ensure he got going he would get distracted and end up hanging around another hour.

"Sure. Gimme a sec."

He bounded up the stairs and into his office. The second floor would serve as his private office and a conference room. The lobby, other offices, and a small kitchen-turned-employee-lounge would take up the downstairs space. Assuming he ever had any employees. Monday morning he would interview receptionist candidates. He had three applicants so far.

The blinking red light on his answering machine signaled that he had at least one message.

Anticipation roiled through him as he pressed the button. He waited through the announcement that he had two new messages. The first was from Renee

Vaughn, a former assistant district attorney from Atlanta. They had spoken by phone yesterday. She was interested in a position at his firm. He was definitely interested in her.

"Mr. Colby," her voice rang out with the strength only a real fighter possessed, "this is Renee Vaughn. I've decided to fly in for a face-to-face before I make a final decision. I'm hoping two-thirty on Monday will work for you. Call my cell if anything comes up." She rattled off the number and the call ended.

"One down and two to go," Jim murmured. His goal was to start out with three associates. He hesitated to call them investigators. The work they would do here wouldn't always involve investigating, at least not in the usual sense.

"Mr. Colby, this is Spencer Anders," floated from the answering machine next. The noise in the background told him Spencer had still been at the bar when he called. At least he'd called.

Jim resisted the urge to shout "yes!"

"I've been thinking about your offer and I'd like to talk to you again. I'll come by your office Monday morning about nine…if you're still interested…. We'll go from there and see what happens."

His trepidation was crystal-clear, but Jim had no doubts. Anders was exactly the kind of associate he wanted on his team. He'd have to thank Lucas for tipping him off to the guy's availability. That Anders had reacted so quickly, if not decisively, indicated an underlying desire to get his life back on track.

A big load off his shoulders, Jim headed down to rendezvous with Victoria. This news gave him something to celebrate at the family dinner tonight.

"Ready?" Victoria asked as he joined her in the soon-to-be lobby.

"I am now." He followed his mother out the front door and locked up.

"I see you've officially hung your shingle."

This was a kind of running joke between them now that he'd actually started classes at the University of Chicago last semester. Taking only one or two classes at a time, completion of the program would require years and years. He was prepared to accept the wait. No matter how long it took he wanted to obtain his law degree. The goal meant a lot to him and even though his mother would never say so, he knew that accomplishment would mean a lot to her as well. She insisted that he was perfect just as he was, but then, she was his mother. His wife was extremely pleased as well.

Jim glanced up at the brand-new sign he'd hung next to the front entrance. Pride welled in his chest. He had made this happen, with a lot of support from the people he loved. "Yep, it's official now."

The Equalizers were about to open for business.

Chapter Two

Monday, February 21

Spencer Anders remained in his car for an additional twenty minutes. He'd made up his mind. The hesitation was unnecessary, but here he sat. Nine-fifteen. He'd told Colby he'd be in around nine.

Why the hell had he done that? The impulse had hit him less than half an hour after Colby had walked out of the joint that had been Spencer's second home since he'd arrived in the Windy City. He used the pay phone at the end of the bar and made the call.

What the hell had he been thinking?

That he had to get his life back? That somehow, things had to start making sense again before he lost himself completely?

Yes to both of the above.

Spencer moistened his lips and fought back the craving for a drink. One didn't go with the other. If he was going to make this work he had to keep his head together.

He could do it.

He banished the nagging voice that tried to tell him otherwise.

"No going backward," he muttered. This was his chance to go forward again. He couldn't screw it up.

Spencer climbed out of the car. He glanced first left then right before crossing the street. He didn't know that much about Jim Colby, but he did know the Colby Agency's esteemed reputation.

He didn't fully understand Jim's decision to start his own firm rather than working at his mother's prestigious agency, but he did trust Lucas Camp.

The name reverberated through him. He'd never actually met the man, but he knew the name, and that was more than sufficient. Five years was a long time. The mission was one of those unwinnable situations where no one was going to walk away satisfied. Still, the mission was crucial. There had been only two members of Spencer's team left by the time a special unit was brought in to attempt a rescue.

Mission Recovery.

Spencer had never heard of the unit. Some black-ops organization loosely attached to the CIA, he'd learned later. Lucas Camp had been the deputy director.

Lucas Camp's unit had saved Spencer's life and the lives of his two remaining team members. If this gig panned out, Spencer would owe Lucas Camp for saving his hide yet a second time.

Maybe he would get the opportunity to thank him in person. Spencer had no idea how the hell Lucas Camp knew he was in Chicago. No, wait. That wasn't true. Camp had been, probably still was, even if only in an advisory capacity, attached to the CIA. Getting intimate information about the Pope himself wouldn't be a problem for a man like him.

Spencer had to admit, having anyone vouch for him these days was a plus. Maybe the whole world didn't see him as a traitor.

That same old fury started to burn deep in his gut. He suppressed the triggered feelings. Thinking about the past would be detrimental to the present, not to mention the future. He had to make a clean break.

That time was now.

He paused at the door to consider the sign. The Equalizers. Interesting moniker. He considered what Colby had told him in their brief meeting. His target client base was those whose troubles couldn't be resolved so easily within the boundaries of the law. He wondered what would make a man like Jim Colby veer that close to criminal activity. From what Spencer knew, the Colby Agency had an impeccable reputation, one respected by clients and law enforcement alike. What made the one and only son of the owner of that esteemed agency different?

Secrets of his own, Spencer surmised. Maybe he

and Colby had something in common—a history best left in the past.

Spencer braced himself and reached for the door. Now or never. This was his chance to start over. He couldn't let it get away. He owed it to himself.

Taking into account the fact that he would otherwise have died five years ago, he owed it to Lucas Camp. He just hoped like hell that he had still had it in him to live up to the man's recommendation.

A new kind of enthusiasm kindled inside him. Jim Colby had told him that his mother was now married to Lucas Camp. If Lucas had recommended him, that meant he wanted Spencer working with Jim. So, he could look at this from the standpoint that not only would he be doing himself a favor by getting his life back together, he'd also be doing Camp a favor. A bit of a stretch, but, hey, it wasn't completely implausible.

Not only was it plausible, the concept served as plenty of motivation for doing this right.

Inside the brownstone, the lobby area was deserted. A desk and a couple of chairs. No receptionist or waiting clients. The decorating reminded him of most military offices, unremarkable and rather drab. Not a problem. After graduating college he'd spent ten years in the army he'd loved. Drab was a preferred color.

Tension rippled through him and Spencer drew in a deep breath before ordering himself to stay calm.

He already knew Colby wanted him on his team. The rest would be nothing more than technicalities. This wasn't an interview, it was a negotiation.

The smell of fresh-brewed coffee wafted from somewhere down the hall. Spencer had about decided to head that way when Jim Colby appeared.

"Right on time." He raised his steaming cup. "Coffee?"

"Coffee would be good." Spencer had already downed three cups but he could definitely use another. The caffeine helped him battle the need for additional fortification. What he now had to consider forbidden fortification.

"Follow me."

Colby led the way to a small kitchen that Spencer presumed would serve as an employee lounge. Refrigerator, microwave, sink and a couple of cabinets. His would-be employer passed him a brimming mug.

"Thanks." The coffee tasted as good as it smelled.

"My office is upstairs."

Spencer nodded and followed Colby to the second floor. Though the brownstone's decor hadn't been updated in a couple of decades, the architecture made it comfortable and interesting in a classic sort of way. The location wasn't one of the most desired in the city, but the neighborhood appeared in the early stages of revitalization. A year or two from now and the streets would be teeming with thriving businesses and highly sought-after lofts. Colby's selection of the location was probably a strategic one.

A sleek wooden desk and leather chair, along with a couple of upholstered chairs for clients, were already stationed in Colby's office. Unpacked boxes of office equipment as well as supplies were scattered about, along with the necessary filing cabinets. Looked as if the boss was well on his way to settling in.

"I'm still getting organized," Colby said as he took the chair behind his desk. "I'll be interviewing receptionists this morning. I hope we'll have someone to answer the phone by lunchtime."

We. Anticipation spiked before Spencer could stop the possibly premature reaction. "What's your current body count?" Might as well get a handle on the personnel arrangement and chain of command before he made any kind of commitment beyond this impulsive appearance.

"So far, two. Me," Colby said with a pointed look at him, "and you."

His answer surprised Spencer. So he really was getting in on the ground floor of a new venture. "What's your operational plan?" Learning the exact nature of what he was getting into here was the first order of business. He wasn't about to be caught off guard again in this lifetime.

"I hope to hire at least three associates."

Associates. Not investigators. This nudged Spencer's curiosity.

"What types of cases do you plan to take on?" The answer to this question was key in many ways. The clientele at any firm was the primary factor in how the firm was judged by others. Though he seriously doubted that Lucas Camp would recommend him for a position within a firm that wasn't on the up and up, Spencer hadn't missed the look in Jim Colby's eyes when he'd talked about helping those whose troubles went beyond the law's boundaries.

"Pretty much whatever walks through the door." Colby set his coffee aside. "In the beginning it may be necessary to take cases we'll choose not to take later on. Right now our primary objective is to get our name out there. To let people know we've set up shop. This business thrives on word of mouth more so than any other means."

Made sense. "What's the plan on case authority? Will you expect to be kept in the loop on all decisions relative to a case once it's assigned?"

"When we take on a client, I'll make a decision as to who is the best man for the job. If it's your case, I'll expect you to lay out a plan of action and then keep me up to speed on how it's coming along. Otherwise, the ultimate moment-to-moment decisions are yours to make."

Spencer nodded. Sounded fair to him. "What about salary?" Since Colby's business was just getting off the ground he wondered how lucrative a proposition this could possibly be.

"We'll all be working for the same base salary, including me," Jim explained. "Whatever profits we net, we'll split evenly among the associates."

Now there was an answer he hadn't expected. "Like a partnership?" Surely that wasn't what he meant. No firm allowed the new hires to start out as equal partners.

"Exactly. We'll all share the burden of cost and we'll all share the bounty."

Once he'd absorbed that surprising response, Spencer moved on to his next question. "Do you have other associates in mind already?"

"I'll be interviewing a candidate this afternoon. If I'm lucky, she'll be coming on board also."

A woman. Spencer had wondered about that as well.

"Renee Vaughn," Jim went on. "She's a former assistant district attorney from Atlanta."

At one time Spencer had considered a law degree. He'd gotten his bachelor's degree in political science, but he'd opted for the military instead of law school. Maybe that had been his first mistake.

"I have an office set up for you," Jim said, dragging Spencer from his unproductive thoughts. "If you're prepared to get started this morning, I'd like you to work up a history for me. Cover your basic skills, any specialized training and the locations where you've worked or been assigned. I'll keep a file like this on all associates for use in determining what cases each is best suited for."

Made sense.

Spencer stood. "Show me the way and I'll get right on it."

Accepting his statement as a yes, Jim nodded. "All right then."

The associates' offices were located on the first floor along the corridor just past the lounge. There were four small offices and a room Jim indicated would be a supply room. At the end of the corridor was the building's rear exit that led into an alley that would serve as a personnel parking area.

As the first associate hired, Spencer got his pick of the offices. He opted for the one on the left side of the hall next to the lounge since it had a window with a view of the neighborhood park across the street.

When the first receptionist candidate arrived for her interview Jim left him to get started on a detailed work history. Typically, that came first, in the form of a résumé, but this situation appeared to be hardly typical.

Maybe that was the reason Spencer felt at home for the first time in more than two years. He'd learned that he couldn't count on anything typical or run-of-the-mill. The everyday was no longer reliable.

Do not go down that road.

All he had to do was keep his eyes forward. No looking back. There was no undoing the past, no matter how wrong. His military career was over. Period. He had an opportunity for something new here. He had to keep that goal in mind if he was to have a future. At the rate he'd been going that prospect had grown pretty dim of late. But that was behind him now.

No looking back.

1:00 p.m.

WILLOW HARRIS sat in her rental car for over half an hour. Most of that time was spent attempting to work up the nerve to make the first move. It wasn't that she was afraid for her safety. The neighborhood wasn't that great, but it wasn't any worse than the one in East St. Louis where her former P.I.'s office was located.

Waiting…working up her courage, she did a lot of that lately. In the beginning sheer adrenaline had driven her, overriding any second thoughts or hesitancy. She'd pushed and pushed and searched and searched without the first consideration for her safety or anything else.

But it was different now.

Another anxiety stalked her like a ruthless killer in the dark.

Fear.

The fear of dashed hope. Each time she moved on to a new investigator her anticipation of finally getting her son back renewed…only to be sucked completely out of her when failure crashed down upon her shoulders all over again.

She'd spent all weekend attempting to locate someone who might be able to help her. Her gaze focused on the street in front of her car. The story had been basically the same with each agency she'd called.

I'm very sorry, Ms. Harris, but that's a case we don't feel comfortable taking on.

Just when she'd been ready to give up, the last guy she'd called—a low-rent one-man operation she'd almost skipped over in her online Yellow Pages search—had told her about a rumor he'd heard. A new shop was opening up in Chicago. There was a buzz going around that this one would be different from all the others.

So here she was, in Chicago sitting outside a place that might very well be her last hope.

The Equalizers.

Her low-rent P.I. had waxed on about how this place planned to take covert investigations to the next level. The Equalizers would accept the less desirable or riskier jobs that no one else wanted to touch.

Since the firm had only just opened, Willow couldn't be sure if the plan to take on any and all cases was out of necessity or not, but she was here.

She was desperate.

Her savings and investments were dwindling fast. This place might very well prove her final hope in more ways than one. There wouldn't be enough money to hire anyone new if this one failed.

An ache twisted through her, making her want to curl up into a ball of defeat. No. She had to be strong.

The only way she would ever get her son back was if she didn't give up, if she tried harder.

Determination rushed through her on the tail of a burst of adrenaline when Davenport's words echoed in her brain. Maybe she *was* looking for a miracle. Who said there was anything wrong with that? Miracles manifested themselves in many ways. She'd been taught that concept her whole life. That was one part of her upbringing she needed to hang onto.

Willow got out of the car and strode across the street to the entrance of the brownstone designated as number 129. The painted wooden sign hanging next to the door announced the name of the business in bold strokes.

The Equalizers.

Well, she would just see if the firm could live up to its fledgling reputation.

Acting before she could think of another reason to waver, she opened the door and went inside. The sudden warmth reminded her that she'd gotten cold sitting in her car with the engine turned off for all that time. A winter chill had blasted the midwest last night, causing major delays in several airports. Thank goodness Midland hadn't been one of them. Once she'd made up her mind to come, she would have done so even if she'd had to walk.

A receptionist sat behind an L-shaped desk. Her back was turned to the door while she typed away at her computer. Several chairs and accompanying tables bordered the room. Magazines were fanned across the top of one of the tables. No plants or goldfish tanks. No heavy stench of cigarette smoke as she'd encountered in many of the agencies she'd visited. Just empty and quiet, like Davenport's office had been, except for the receptionist's busy fingers on the keyboard.

The decorating scheme left something to be desired, but the place was neat and clean. She could appreciate that after the last couple of places she'd visited in the past forty-eight hours.

Since the receptionist didn't make the usual overture though she'd surely heard the door close, Willow stepped closer to her desk and spoke up. "My name is Willow Harris. I'm here to see the man in charge." She purposely left off the phrase *if he's available*. She'd come too far to accept any kind of excuse. The idea that he could be out of town banded around her chest and squeezed. Booking the first available flight and rushing here might have been a mistake, but she'd had no choice.

Her situation wouldn't wait. She'd waited too long already.

Please let him be here.

Rather than offer a customary greeting, the receptionist frowned as she gave Willow a thorough once-over with assessing brown eyes. She appeared less than pleased at being interrupted from whatever she'd been doing on the computer. Maybe she wasn't the receptionist at all. She could be one of the investigators who had decided to use this computer for one reason or the other.

"Is he in?" Willow prompted after another awkward moment elapsed. And here she had thought she'd already seen the most bizarre and unprofessional this business had to offer.

"How do you know the person in charge isn't a woman?" The woman tucked a handful of sandy-brown hair behind one ear and gave Willow a pointed look.

Too taken aback to be embarrassed, Willow struggled a moment to come up with an appropriate response. "Well…who *is* in charge?" Maybe this woman didn't work here at all.

"Mr. Jim Colby," the woman behind the desk said with a smile that wasn't really a smile, more a fleeting tick. "Do you have an appointment?"

Willow looked around the small reception area. There was no one else there. Unless Mr. Colby already had a client in his office or was expecting one momentarily, she didn't see the point in the question. But then she remembered the discreet way Davenport had operated.

"No," she admitted. "I don't have an appointment. I flew in from St. Louis this morning in hopes that Mr. Colby could make some time for me."

"Calling first would have been smarter."

Willow reminded herself that she needed to get

past this woman and to the man in charge. Giving her any advice on how a proper receptionist conducted herself might not be conducive to making that happen.

The truth was the woman was right. But Willow managed to keep her voice calm. "I know. I apologize for just showing up like this, but the matter is urgent."

The receptionist, who didn't wear a name badge or have a name plate on her desk and who looked utterly unimpressed, smiled another of those unsmiles. "I'm new here. I'll have to check his calendar first." She flipped through the calendar taking up space on the oak desktop next to the telephone. Not a single page she previewed had anything at all written on it.

"He appears to be free," the receptionist announced. "Just have a seat, Ms. Harris, and I'll find out if he can see you today." She gestured to a chair.

Willow settled into a chair and tried to slow her mind's frantic churning. Exhaustion simply wasn't an adequate description of just how tired she felt. It was, however, the only word she could think of at the moment. This man—Jim Colby—had to help her.

The receptionist buzzed her boss on the intercom, using the handset to keep his end of the conversation private. A couple of pauses and yes sirs, and then she placed the handset back in its cradle.

"Up the stairs and the first door on the left."

Evidently that was a yes to the question of whether or not he was available. Willow offered a polite smile, deserved or not. "Thank you."

The woman didn't say anything, not even a "You're welcome." She swiveled in her chair and resumed her work at the computer. Mr. Colby needed to seriously consider public relations classes for his receptionist.

The desperation clawing at Willow's heart was the only thing that kept her from walking out, considering the vibes she'd gotten so far. If she'd wasted the money coming here…if she'd made a mistake…

She blocked the thoughts. Stay focused. There hadn't been any other choice. This was her last hope.

A man she presumed to be Jim Colby waited in the doorway of an office in the upstairs corridor.

"Ms. Harris." He thrust out his hand. "I'm Jim Colby."

She placed her hand in his and he gave it a firm shake. "Thank you for seeing me, Mr. Colby."

"Can I get you some coffee or water?" He directed her into his office as he made the offer.

Expansive oak desk, a credenza and lots of file cabinets along with numerous unpacked boxes took up most of the floor space in the office. Mr. Colby had, literally, just set up shop. "Ah…no, thank you," she abruptly remembered to say in answer to his question. Though she appreciated that he appeared determined to be polite, getting right down to business was her priority at the moment. She sat down in one of the upholstered chairs and waited for him to do the same on the other side of his desk.

He studied her a moment, intense blue eyes looking right through her as if she were an open book published in easy-to-read large print. His assessment, however, appeared far less suspicious than that of his receptionist.

"What can I do for you, Ms. Harris?"

This was the hard part. How did she adequately relay the volatility and urgency of her situation as concisely as possible?

"It all started four years ago," she began, without allowing the gut-wrenching memories that attempted to bob to the surface to do so. She'd learned long ago not to revisit that past. It was too hard to maintain her sanity otherwise. "I was traveling on business in Kuwait. I met a man and we had a…sort of whirlwind romance. We married only a few days later."

She didn't see any reason to give him the trivial details of her lapse into stupidity. She'd relived those days over and over again already in an attempt to pinpoint something—anything—that should have served as a warning to her. So far she'd found nothing.

"Two years ago we had a child, a boy."

Something in his expression changed when she said *boy*. She already knew what he was thinking. A boy was a far more prized asset than a girl, even in a country as liberal and progressive as the State of Kuwait, making her quest a far more difficult one.

"Eight months ago I realized I couldn't live the

way my husband wanted me to for a moment longer." It was not nearly as simple as that, but she knew from experience that he would ask questions until he had all the information he needed. No need to go into the gory details until she knew whether he intended to take her case or not. "I decided that a divorce was the only option. I could return to my home in the States and put those years in the Middle East behind me."

"But your ex didn't want you to take his son out of the country."

Before she could stop the onslaught, memories from that day swarmed inside her head, making her want to cry. She blinked back the emotions. This might be her last chance. She couldn't screw it up.

"Not only did he not want me to take him out of Kuwait, he wanted me to go and he never wanted me to see my child again." How could she have lived with him for nearly three years and not noticed how little he actually cared for her? She'd gotten a crash course those last few months.

Focus, Willow. No drifting.

Jim Colby waited for her to continue. She licked her lips, swallowed at the emotion pressing at the back of her throat and said the rest. "He had me exported out of the country like black-market cargo. He left me at an airport in California with no ID at all. He took everything to ensure I couldn't immediately return. Then he filed for divorce and claimed I had deserted him as well as our son."

"The Kuwaiti legal system ruled in his favor, of course."

She nodded, unsure of her voice now. Images of her little boy kept swimming in front of her eyes.

"When was the last time you saw your son, Ms. Harris?"

"Eight months, one week and two days ago." She could give him the actual hour, but she'd given enough.

"Why seek professional help now? After so many months? Did your attorney give you reason to believe your situation could be worked out some other way?"

He cut right to the chase. She liked that. Hope glimmered inside her.

"I started with the legal system. But I soon figured out that I wasn't going to make this happen through legal channels. My lawyer was pretty up-front about that. Then I started hiring private investigators in an attempt to find someone who could help me."

"How many P.I.s have you hired during the past few months?"

She wanted to tell him that information was irrelevant. But he was right to ask. He couldn't operate unless he had all the pertinent facts. Going through half a dozen P.I.s had taught her that.

"Six."

He was number seven if she didn't count the low-rent guy who had given her the free advice about coming here.

If the number surprised him he didn't let on. But

she wasn't so sure she would be able to read anything in those blue eyes anyway. If she'd thought Davenport was unreadable, this guy had it down to a science.

"What is it you want me to do for you, Ms. Harris?"

Not only could she not read his eyes, his voice gave away absolutely nothing.

She clutched the arms of her chair, braced herself for an uphill battle. "I just want my son back, Mr. Colby. I don't care how you have to do it. I want him back."

"You're certain he's still alive and living in Kuwait?"

The question, uttered with such frankness, tore at her heart. But at least it wasn't a no. That meant he was considering her request.

"Yes, I'm positive."

Now would come the part that would change his mind.

"Tell me about your ex-husband. Is he the kind of man who would go to extreme measures to keep what he believed belonged to him? What kind of personal security, if any, does he maintain?"

Ice slid through her veins. This was where he would insert the "no."

"My ex-husband will do anything to keep his son." She thought of Davenport's man and a new wave of terror washed over her. She had to tell that part to Colby. "Including possibly hurting anyone who gets in his way. He has a heavy security detail." Davenport had used those terms when describing her husband's personal security.

Please, God, she prayed, *don't let this man be afraid to take her case.*

The strangest thing happened then. Mr. Colby smiled. Not the wide, ear-to-ear kind of charming smile to set her at ease. Not at all. This quirk of his lips was one-sided, almost daring. She hadn't noticed the scar on his cheek until then. The scar had her looking closer...noting the harsh planes and angles of his face. He looked hard...brutal maybe. Fear trickled through her. Whatever it takes, she reminded herself.

"Sounds like your ex-husband needs a lesson in proper parenting. Not to worry, Ms. Harris, I know how to handle men like him."

She blinked, took a breath to banish the trepidation that had started to build. Had she misunderstood?

"Does this mean you're taking my case?"

"I'm not only taking your case, Ms. Harris, I'm going to get your son back for you."

Chapter Three

6:20 p.m.

Over three hours.

Willow had left Jim Colby's office at three o'clock. He'd promised to call as soon as he was prepared to brief her on his strategy for recovering her son.

She'd checked into a motel close by. She'd been waiting ever since.

Her cell phone lay on the bedside table, the charging icon blinking. She'd almost forgotten to plug it in. That would have been bad. That portable device had become her lifeline in the past few months. She never knew when the P.I. currently working her case would need to reach her, so she'd kept the thing turned on 24/7.

She thought about Jim Colby and his insistence that he would ensure she got her son back. That was definitely a first. She'd had several ambitious P.I.s claim they could handle her case upon initial acceptance, but not one had looked her dead in the eye and stated unequivocally that he would get the job done.

A blend of hope and uncertainty twisted in her chest. Could Jim Colby really do this?

Who was this man who would dare to make such a promise?

Before coming to Chicago she had looked up what she could about him on the Internet, but most of the stuff that had popped up on her search was actually about his mother and her private investigations agency. His past appeared to have fallen beneath the radar somehow. Whether that was good or bad she hadn't decided just yet.

But if he could get her son back she didn't care what lay behind that slightly marred, flinty face. Who he was didn't really matter. All that mattered was whether or not he could do what he said he could do.

She wanted desperately to cling to that hope, but she needed to know more before she let herself believe fully in this man. However prestigious his mother's reputation, he was an unknown and unproven entity.

God, she was so tired. She'd barely slept last night. As much as she wanted to crash and sleep for hours, she couldn't do that until she had some indication of what would happen next.

...you're looking for a miracle...

Maybe Davenport had been right. Maybe she *was* looking for a miracle. She'd certainly had the kind recounted in the Bible told to her over and over again as a child, but did real miracles actually happen anymore? And the next question was, had she found that miracle, if it really did exist, in the Equalizers?

A knock on the door of her motel room had her practically jumping out of her skin.

Housekeeping? Surely not at this hour. No one knew she was in Chicago. Not that she had anyone. Even her folks had disowned her when she married someone they considered a terrorist. That had been the kinder of the names they had given him.

Evidently they had been right after all. Certainly *devil* came to her mind whenever she thought of her ex these days.

A second knock jerked her back from the preoccupation that total exhaustion allowed to creep up on her so easily and at the least likely moments.

She stood. Smoothed a hand over her skirt and walked as quietly as she could to the door. Pressing her eye to the peephole she resisted the urge to draw away in surprise or fear or possibly both as her brain registered the stranger standing on the other side of the door.

Male. Thirty or thirty-two maybe.

Tall, strong-looking.

Uneasiness coursed through her veins.

This had to be a mistake. He had to have stopped at the wrong room.

Should she say something? But then he'd know she was in here…alone. Why hadn't she bought pepper spray months ago? Coming here like this—doing all she'd done over the past eight months—was more than enough reason to be concerned with protecting herself.

The trouble was she hadn't been thinking about anyone except her son. Dumb, Willow. What good would she be to her son if she got herself killed?

"Ms. Harris?"

Willow took a big step back from the door.

How could this stranger know her name?

"Ms. Harris, my name is Spencer Anders. Jim Colby sent me to discuss your case."

She allowed herself to breathe. Jim Colby. Okay. But why would he send someone to her motel? Had she even told Mr. Colby where she'd be staying?

For a moment she couldn't think, then she remembered. Yes, she'd left word. She'd called the receptionist and provided the name and address of the motel where she could be reached. After her experience with the receptionist, Willow hadn't been sure whether Mr. Colby would get the message or not. Evidently he had.

She stepped to the door once more. "Do you have identification?" She cleared her throat, annoyed at the tremble in her voice. New concerns immediately started to surface. Why wasn't Mr. Colby handling her case himself? He was the one to insist he could get her son back. Was this his way of copping out? If his man failed would Colby be off the hook for making such a claim so hastily?

Willow closed her eyes and fought the vertigo of fear and confusion. She had to stop this. She had to focus.

She opened her eyes and watched through the tiny hole as the man who had identified himself as Spencer Anders reached into his hip pocket and withdrew a wallet. When he held a Louisiana driver's license up for her to see she confirmed that his name was indeed Spencer Anders.

"Why do you have a Louisiana driver's license?" Relevant or not she wanted to know. Louisiana was an awfully long way from Illinois. If he was a licensed P.I. in Illinois, wouldn't he need to be a resident of this state? Too many questions that just didn't matter. She was borrowing trouble and putting off the inevitable.

"I'm new to Chicago." He slid the license back into his wallet, then tucked the wallet into his pocket once more. "Look, Ms. Harris, if you're uncomfortable speaking to me in your room, I'll wait for you in the coffee shop down the block."

Maybe she should call Jim Colby and confirm that he'd sent this man.

"We've worked out the strategy for recovering your son," Anders said, drawing her attention back to him. "If you're still interested in hearing the details, I'll be waiting in the coffee shop. Take a left at the motel entrance and you can't miss it."

...recovering your son...

Willow wrenched the door open when he started to walk away. "Wait."

He hesitated a moment before turning to face her. A new trickle of trepidation slithered down her spine. Stop it, she ordered. This man was here to help her. Getting off on the wrong foot wouldn't be productive.

He faced her and only then did she actually look at him closely enough to absorb the details. Dark hair, really dark. Gray eyes. Tired eyes. His expression wasn't precisely grim, but the lines and angles of his face spoke of having seen more unpleasantness than any one human was built to take. Just like his employer.

His height, six-one at least, put her off just a little. At five-two, she found that almost everyone was taller than her. Perhaps it was the broad shoulders that went along with the towering height, coupled with the grim face that unsettled her just a little. No, she decided, it was the eyes. Somber. Weary. The eyes looked way older than the thirty-one or -two he appeared to be. And yet there was a keen alertness staring out at her from those solemn depths.

What she saw or didn't see was of no consequence. He was here. He had a plan. That was the whole point...the only point.

"Come in." She squared her shoulders and told herself to get past the hesitation. All this attempting to read between the lines was making her paranoid. She'd never met Davenport's man, the one who'd probably lost his life while getting close to her son. For all she knew he might have been far more intimidating than this man.

Willow moved away from the door to allow Anders entrance. After coming inside he closed the door, but remained standing directly in front of it.

Taking a deep, steadying breath, she opened the conversation. The next move was clearly hers. "Thank you for coming, Mr. Anders." That was a mega understatement, but it would suffice. She could thank him properly when he'd gotten her son back.

"I have a few questions for you, Ms. Harris." He reached into an interior pocket of his leather jacket. "The information you provided was helpful, but I need more details to round out our strategy."

Jim Colby had asked her to make a list of the events that had led up to her decision to ask for a divorce from her husband, as well as anything she could think of related to him or his family that might be useful in the coming task. She'd spent an hour coming up with as many details as she could call to mind. Mr. Colby had obviously passed her list along to Mr. Anders.

Might as well get comfortable. If this went anything like her interviews with previous investigators, it would take some time.

"Please." She indicated the chair next to the small table positioned in front of the window. "Sit." She perched on the edge of the bed and tugged at the hem of her skirt to ensure it stayed close to her knees where it belonged. She cleared her mind of any static prompted by worry or anxiety as she clasped her hands in her lap and waited for him to begin. Listening carefully was essential in understanding the details.

As he took the seat she'd offered, she focused on the man in an effort to get a fix on him. First, she considered the way he dressed. The leather bomber jacket was brown and had the worn appearance of being a favorite. The blue jeans were equally faded and obviously a favored wardrobe selection as well. The black V-neck sweater he wore beneath the jacket was layered on top of a white T-shirt, both of which looked new. If she had to assess him solely on his overall appearance she would conclude that he was a nice man with a lot of painful history.

Willow abruptly wondered if he came to the same conclusion about her. Nice, with a heavy load of hurt slung around her neck like a millstone.

"Did you sign any kind of legal documents when you married Mr. al-Shimmari? A prenuptial agreement or other binding arrangement? Anything at all besides a marriage license?"

Willow regarded his question carefully before shaking her head. There had been essentially no paperwork involved. "Nothing. I know it sounds strange now, but we really were in love. Or, at least, I was. I had no money, other than my salary and a few small investments, and he didn't appear worried that I would attempt to steal any of his." She'd already been down this road with her attorney during the divorce proceedings. There was nothing to be gained by rehashing it, but she kept that to herself. She needed to give this man a chance.

"Did he or his family pressure you to convert to the ways of Islam?"

A frown tugged at her forehead, the tension somehow reaching all the way to the base of her skull. This was one she hadn't been asked before. "No. Not really. It was suggested a couple of times, but he knew I wasn't going to convert when we married. We talked about that. He didn't have a problem with my decision."

Spencer Anders leaned forward and braced his elbows on his knees. "Ms. Harris, do you know if your ex-husband was Sunni or Shia?"

She wasn't sure where he was going with this. "Sunni." His hands kept distracting her. They hung between his spread thighs, relaxed but infinitely dangerous-looking. A person's hands said a lot about them. She'd always been fascinated by hands. She blinked, forced her eyes to meet his and her brain to get back on track. "Why?"

Those gray eyes searched hers as if he needed to be sure she didn't already know the answer he was about to give her. What was it he thought he knew that she didn't? Apprehension started its dreaded rise once more.

"According to the laws of his country and his religion, he could marry you without consequence. He could have children with you and retain full custody in the event you divorced—under one condition."

She'd learned about that law the hard way. Her attorney hadn't been able to find any exceptions or conditions. "What condition?" If what he was about to tell her impacted his ability to help her get her son back…maybe she didn't want to know.

"That you didn't convert. A non-Muslim woman cannot be granted custody of any child, girl or boy, when divorcing a Muslim man. You didn't need a pre-nup because as a non-Muslim you weren't entitled to any property or money. That's the law, Ms. Harris. You never had a leg to stand on."

He was right. This part was definitely no surprise to her. "I found that out too late." She should have been smarter. But she'd been in love. The idea that Khaled had urged her to retain her own beliefs for underhanded purposes sent fury roaring through her even now. He'd insisted that he was perfectly happy without her bothering with conversion. She'd considered his understanding an act of love and trust. Lies. All of it. His assurances had all been for one thing alone—to guarantee he couldn't lose any children they might have.

There was just one thing about the way the marriage ended that didn't sit right with that scenario. Her attorney hadn't been able to give her an answer to that question. "Since the law protected his right to custody, why ship me out of the country so secretively?" He'd kidnapped her off the street and sent her to L.A. with two of his goons. They'd left her there, with no money and no ID. It had been a nightmare. Why had he bothered? Was the act meant to humiliate her? To frighten her? That he'd later denied it only added insult to injury.

"To justify his claims of desertion," Anders offered as if that answer should be crystal-clear. "Though you had no right to custody, you could have challenged the divorce as long as he had no legal grounds against you. Dumping you back on American soil made you look like the bad guy and gave him exactly what he needed—legal grounds to support his accusations and sympathy."

Anders was right. Why hadn't she thought of that? She'd been duped from the beginning, but this last was the ultimate betrayal. He'd charmed and seduced her, then tied her hands with sweet words of understanding.

How stupid and blind she'd been.

"So what do we do?" She appreciated that he had been able to clear up that question when her attorney hadn't been able to, but she needed more. She needed this man to lay out a plan that would ensure her son's safe return to her.

The sooner the better.

For one long beat she held her breath. Whether it was the cool distance she saw in his eyes or the apprehension compounding inside her, overriding her momentary burst of anger, she was afraid to breathe. She needed him to say he could make this happen.

"I have more questions related to your ex-husband's family and living arrangements as well as his financial dealings. It's essential that I have as much information as you can give me before walking into this situation. Information is power, Ms. Harris. The more I have, the better prepared I am to accomplish my mission."

"You'll be going to Kuwait, not Mr. Colby?" That she sounded disappointed was not lost on him. She hoped that wouldn't prove a strike against her, but she was a little disappointed. Jim Colby had been so sure he could get her son back. Was this man capable of the same promise?

"I'll be handling your case," Anders verified. To his credit he kept any resentment at her question out of his voice as well as his expression.

She'd let her feelings be known, no point beating around the bush about her bottom line. "Can you make the same guarantee Mr. Colby made?" She needed his reassurance. More than he could possibly fathom. This was far too important for her to be dancing around the issue.

Spencer wasn't sure he should answer this woman's question the way he would prefer. Jim Colby had put him in an awkward position. Yes, Spencer was relatively certain he could make this happen. He'd spent a decade in covert operations and a good deal of that time in the Middle East. He knew how to get in, accomplish his mission and get out. Not a problem.

But this wasn't as cut-and-dried as a military operation. And it damned sure wasn't black or white.

This was a child. A small boy, whose life and future hung in the balance.

As good as Spencer was, and he was very good at his job, stuff happened. A stray gunshot, unexpected extra manpower in a standoff—way more variables than he had time to contemplate could come into play. It wasn't as simple as going in, nabbing the child and getting out.

Khaled al-Shimmari wasn't just your run-of-the-mill Middle-Eastern rich guy. The man had connections, major connections. His family was extremely powerful, more so, Spencer felt certain, than this lady suspected. He didn't see any reason to go into that with her just now.

There was one glaring detail in particular he planned to keep to himself for the moment: the fact that her ex was suspected of supporting terrorism. Spencer had logged into certain FBI files with the help of the new receptionist Jim had hired. She might not have much personality, but she could hack into anything. That skill could be very useful and at the same time extremely dangerous. But that was Colby's problem, not Spencer's.

Willow Harris stared at him expectantly. She wanted an answer to her question. Yes or no. He understood what she was looking for.

"I can tell you that I have extensive experience in

the Middle East. I'm former military and my unit specialized in hostage retrieval. I have a perfect record, no failures whatsoever." He hoped that answered her question without actually answering it. Being evasive wasn't his intent, but he couldn't make her the promise she wanted. Not in good faith anyway. Colby had put him in a hell of a position. Spencer wondered if his new employer really had that much confidence in him or if he was simply that desperate for business.

With her hands wrung together in her lap, she bit her bottom lip and analyzed his response for a moment. He took advantage of that time to do a little analyzing of his own. She was young. Twenty-eight according to his research. She had a degree in marketing with an emphasis on foreign trading. She'd been recruited right out of college with a firm that catered to Middle-Eastern investors.

Willow Harris had no criminal record, not even a parking ticket. She'd graduated college with honors and appeared to be very conservative in behavior and dress. Her navy skirt went all the way to her knees. The white button-up blouse was buttoned all the way up. Silky blond hair fell around her shoulders. She was pretty and clearly too naive for her own good. Those big green eyes watched him now as if he were the only man on earth who could save her from a fate worse than death.

Poor kid. That bastard al-Shimmari had taken total

advantage of her. Spencer had a bad feeling about just who al-Shimmari really was. The fact that he was on the FBI watch list might very well be only the tip of the iceberg.

He had his doubts as to whether this case was as straightforward as it appeared from a distance.

She inhaled a big breath, unintentionally drawing his attention to her lips. Nice lips. Soft, full. Spencer snapped his gaze to hers and gave himself a swift mental kick for being an idiot.

"Your military history is impressive, Mr. Anders." She licked those distracting lips and seemed to struggle with her next words. "Can you…will you tell me why you're no longer in the military? I mean, you look too young to be retired and I…well, I was wondering why a man like you would walk away from such an impressive career."

Not as naive as he'd presumed, apparently. He considered lying to her. He was relatively certain she wouldn't want to hear the truth. But she'd been lied to enough already. Six P.I.s in as many months. Nope. This lady deserved the whole truth.

"My superior officer accused me of being a traitor."

Her pupils flared with surprise.

No turning back now. "He claimed that I sold information about an operation to the enemy. Since he couldn't prove it, I wasn't court-martialed to the degree he'd hoped. There were, however, other lesser charges backed up by supposed eye witnesses. In the end I was charged with insubordination and behavior unbecoming an officer. I was demoted and given the opportunity to start over. I opted not to."

That was the condensed version. It was also all she would get from him.

Even those few sentences had bitterness and fury churning in his gut.

She blinked rapidly, concealing her initial reaction. "Oh."

He knew better than to expect her to be anything other than shocked or appalled, maybe both. And yet he expected more somehow. He was sick and tired of people judging him wrongly for getting screwed by a ranking officer. He hadn't done anything wrong.

But she couldn't know that.

She would only understand one thing: her newest hope for getting her son back had been labeled a possible traitor to his country by the United States Army. That had to be a little scary.

"Well." She cleared her throat delicately and sat up a little straighter, but didn't look directly at him. "Were you…? A traitor…I mean?"

The anger and bitterness rushed out of him in a choked laugh. He had to hand it to the lady, she was original. Instead of ending the meeting and ushering him out, she flat-out asked what was on her mind.

"No. I wasn't a traitor. I just got on the bad side of the wrong jerk, the man who happened to be my commanding officer. He used me as a scapegoat when he couldn't find the real traitor." Spencer had always wondered if his superior had been the real traitor…if the whole setup had been about some sort of vengeance since Spencer had outshone him numerous times. He supposed he would never know.

Willow Harris's expression brightened as she let out an audible sigh. "Good. Now that we have that out of the way, when do we leave?"

"We?" Dread kicked into high gear. This was not a tactic he'd anticipated. Jim Colby certainly hadn't mentioned her desire to be involved with the operation.

She folded her arms over her chest and set her chin to a challenging tilt. "I've decided that this time I want to be involved. Ata is my child. Maybe that was my mistake all along. I should be a part of the operation."

No way that would work. "I'm afraid your presence would only complicate matters, Ms. Harris. You don't have the proper training—"

"This is not negotiable, Mr. Anders." She stared straight into his eyes, hers stone-cold determined. "I will be right there beside you every step of the way, otherwise I'll have to take my business elsewhere."

The last gave Spencer pause. Jim Colby would not be pleased if he screwed this up. He had accepted this case, and he wanted it done. ASAP. He damn sure couldn't expect to stay in business by turning clients away. This job was Spencer's chance to really start over. To build a new life with an employer who seemed to trust him implicitly.

If he tossed away this opportunity…would another one that offered the same come his way?

Not likely.

His hands shook. He could sure use a drink right about now. But that wouldn't solve the problem. Jim Colby was counting on him. Spencer was counting on *himself*.

And this lady—his full attention settled on Willow Harris—was counting on him. She wanted her child back. She deserved her child back.

Spencer pushed aside all the reasons he would be out of his mind to move forward under these terms. "You understand, Ms. Harris, that this mission will be dangerous?" He wanted all the cards on the table. No misconceptions or misunderstandings. "Your presence could actually jeopardize my ability to react as swiftly as I may need to, in effect jeopardizing the whole operation."

The delicate muscles of her long slender throat worked hard as she summoned a response. "I understand the danger. I'm fully prepared to take the risk."

Was she? he wondered. She'd lived in Kuwait for three years or a little better. Did she really comprehend how bad it could be without the support and approval of her ex-husband? He doubted it.

"Just one more question." This one would be the deal-breaker.

Her gaze locked with his. He didn't miss the determination there or the underlying fear. She might want him to believe that she wasn't afraid, but she was. She was very afraid. As she should be.

"If I have to make a choice between saving you or saving the child, I will save the child." He allowed the ramifications of those words to sink in a second or two before he continued. "Are you prepared to die knowing that your death possibly equates to a forfeit?"

Three, four, then five beats passed.

"Yes."

So much for his scare tactics. "In that case," he relented, "we'll begin preparations tomorrow."

Chapter Four

Tuesday, February 22

Spencer spread the map of Kuwait City over his desk and considered his strategy. The major streets ran in east-west rings starting with 1st Ring Road in the heart of the city all the way to 6th Ring near the airport. North-south streets intersected the rings. The al-Shimmari estate sprawled in the Suilhibikat area wedged between 2nd Ring Road and 3rd. This was where most of the wealthy Kuwaiti families resided.

The al-Shimmari residence was twenty thousand square feet protected by towering security walls as well as armed guards. According to his mother, the boy, Ata, was never out of sight of the grandmother, who was extremely possessive, or at least one personal-security guard.

The ex-husband, Khaled, had high-level government connections. Which meant Spencer couldn't risk entering the country accompanied by Ms.

Willow Harris. Before she would have time to clear customs Khaled would know she was in-country.

That one was a no-brainer.

Spencer had been surprised at the kind of connections Jim Colby himself had right here in Chicago. Fake papers for Willow Harris and her son had been as easy to get as filling a prescription at a local pharmacy. The quality of the passports and driver's license was remarkable. He wasn't the slightest bit worried about her papers being flagged, here or there.

What did worry the hell out of him was *her*. His mission would involve getting as close to the target as possible without being noticed by the enemy. He had no doubt that, if given a careful block of instruction, he could count on her full cooperation in whatever capacity he deemed operationally necessary. His primary concern, however, was whether or not she would be able to maintain any sort of objectivity, much less keep a handle on her emotions. Seeing her child again for the first time after so many months would take an immediate toll.

He didn't know her, other than what he'd seen and heard so far, but there was no reason for him to believe that she would behave any differently than any other mother thrust into a situation such as this.

Human emotion had no place in a covert operation.

He had been trained to set aside all emotion and to focus on attaining the target. Willow had no training whatsoever other than in how to negotiate and maneuver stocks and bonds. She was ill-prepared for this operation and, unfortunately, he hadn't come up with a legitimate reason to change her mind about full participation. He had spoken with Jim Colby regarding his reservations about her involvement. Jim had left the ball in his court.

If Spencer didn't think he could accomplish the mission with her in tow, then he could pass with Jim's blessings. Willow Harris would simply have to go elsewhere for help in retrieving her son.

That was the thing, though. Spencer was reasonably sure he could accomplish the mission either way. It was those pesky variables that troubled him. If his or someone else's timing was off, if there were unexpected changes in location or the body count of the enemy…any one of a hundred different scenarios could alter a single reaction, resulting in devastating consequences.

He didn't want to get this woman injured or killed. He'd watched his team members slaughtered on that mission five years ago and he had no desire to go through an encore performance.

Every time he'd thought about telling Willow Harris that he just couldn't take the risk, he remembered the haunting pain in her eyes. The elemental need to hold her child in her arms again. No one should have to go through that kind of agony, especially not alone.

When it came to variables there were plenty, it

seemed, in Willow's personal life, the circumstances with her child aside. She appeared to be completely on her own with no support network. Yet her mother and father, according to his research, were still alive. She drifted from job to job, sticking mainly with temporary agencies for any kind of work for which she possessed the qualifications. She lived in the kind of apartments most people would consider barely a cut above the slums. Evidently most of what she'd earned and/or saved had gone into the pockets of one P.I. after the other. She'd forked over the firm's required retainer fee without blinking an eye. Yet the motel she'd selected was one whose clientele rented more often by the hour than the night.

From all accounts she had sacrificed a great deal in hopes of getting her son back.

Spencer scrubbed his hand over his jaw. Man, he couldn't allow feelings of sympathy to sneak up on him like that. He was real sorry for her troubles, but sympathy, no matter how well-placed, led to trouble. He'd learned that the hard way. He could not—would not—get personally involved on this case or any other.

He had a fresh start here, he wasn't about to let anything or anyone screw it up. He had a job to do, end of story. Feeling sorry for a client wouldn't get the job done. He had to remember that. Allowing emotions to slip in would lead him straight back to his old buddy…booze. No vulnerabilities. If he permitted a single chink in his armor of determination he'd live to regret it.

The intercom on his desk buzzed, followed by the receptionist's voice. "Spencer, your two o'clock is here."

Willow Harris.

He'd told her to come in around two. He'd known it would take most of the morning to pull together the necessary documentation. Next he would lay out his plan for her approval. Moving forward with actual travel plans would be foolhardy prior to getting her on board with his change of identity strategy.

"Thanks, Connie. Send her on back."

"Fine," the receptionist huffed before disconnecting.

Spencer shook his head. He didn't quite get this one. Connie Gardener was extremely intelligent and intensely focused. She was a definite asset when it came to research and planning. But the lady had no people skills. None whatsoever. She'd just as soon tell you to drop dead as to say good morning, depending upon her mood. And that predilection extended to the boss as well as to Spencer or the mailman or anyone else who stuck his or her head through the door. Somehow, Connie just didn't get that she was a receptionist at this firm. Being receptive and polite was part of her job.

Spencer supposed Jim Colby saw beyond her prickly personality to the definite asset beneath. As long as she didn't actually run off any clients, Spencer didn't have a problem with her. Considering most of their clients would likely be as desperate for help as Willow Harris, he doubted even a snarky receptionist would keep those in need away. He had to assume Colby had some reason Spencer didn't know about for hiring and keeping the woman in spite of her lack of tact.

Willow Harris appeared at his open door just then, dragging his attention back to the more pressing problem at hand. She wore another skirt today, this one pink. The hem brushed her knees the same as yesterday's navy one had. Despite the conservative length of the skirt, the straight, slightly narrow fit flattered her petite figure. A pink sweater and sensible brown flats completed her wardrobe. She looked nice if not trendy.

"Good morning, Ms. Harris."

Her lips tilted in the expected expression of politeness, but the smile didn't reach her eyes. "Mr. Anders."

"Have a seat." He indicated the chair in front of his desk. "I was about to get a refill." He picked up his coffee cup. "Would you like a cup? Or maybe a soft drink?"

"Coffee would be nice. Thank you." She took a seat, careful to tug her skirt down as far as it would go before primly crossing her legs.

"I'll be right back." He paused at his door and studied her a moment. With her back to him, he could do so without rousing her suspicion or her questions.

She shifted in her seat a couple of times before she appeared to get comfortable. Her hands trembled once, twice, as she attempted to figure out what to do with them.

As calm as she wanted to appear, she was nervous.

About whether or not he could get the job done? he wondered, doubt creeping in despite his best efforts.

Or was her apprehension related to returning to Kuwait and possibly having to face her former husband?

Spencer turned, his movements soundless, and headed for the small employee lounge. Her apprehension would have to be addressed before they moved forward. He would need to know exactly how she felt and why she felt that way. *She* needed to think long and hard about whether or not she could really handle the coming emotional storm. Nothing about this mission was going to be easy.

"Anders, do you have a moment?"

Spencer turned from the coffeepot at the sound of Jim Colby's voice. His new boss and partner came into the lounge accompanied by a female. Thirty-two, thirty-three. Elegant business suit. Dark hair pulled away from her face, not a single strand out of place.

The prosecutor. What was her name? Oh, yeah. Renee Vaughn. From Atlanta. Colby had mentioned her. She'd come by for an interview yesterday, but Spencer had missed her.

"Sure." Spencer sat his coffee cup aside.

"This is Renee Vaughn from Atlanta. She's joining our team." To the lady, he said, "Anders is former military—Special Forces."

Vaughn thrust out her hand. "It's a pleasure, Mr. Anders."

Spencer gave her hand a shake. She had a firm grip and a definite no-nonsense air about her. "Good to have you on board, Ms. Vaughn."

"Mr. Colby!" Connie shouted unceremoniously. "You've got a call on line one!"

Jim Colby excused himself, leaving Spencer and the newest associate to fill the abrupt silence.

Vaughn jerked her head toward the door. "What's your take on the receptionist?" The humor sparkling in her eyes tipped Spencer off to her amusement with Connie's unrestrained brashness.

"She's one of kind, that's for sure."

"Definitely," Vaughn agreed. "But I hear she's a former computer security analyst. Spent time in federal prison for hacking."

That certainly explained a few things. "Really?" Spencer filled his coffee cup. "I hadn't heard the prison part." Maybe he and Connie had more in common than he'd first imagined.

"She mentioned it to me as soon as I arrived for my interview yesterday. Maybe because I'm a former district attorney. I'm not sure if she thought I should be impressed or was simply warning me." Vaughn shrugged her designer-clad shoulders. "I'll assume both for the moment." Her gaze settled fully on Spencer then. "What about you, Anders?" she asked. "Got any skeletons in your closet?"

"I'll tell you what I do have, Ms. Vaughn," he offered as he reached for a second cup and filled it. "A client waiting in my office. Help yourself to the coffee."

"I'd tell you to call me Renee," she said, reaching for a cup of her own, "but I haven't been called by my first name since law school. You can drop the Ms. though. Vaughn is fine."

"I'll remember that." He didn't wait around for her to ask any more questions. He told himself that he wasn't ashamed of his past; he just didn't want to talk about it with a virtual stranger. But that was probably more lie than truth.

Back in his office, he pushed the door closed with his foot, then passed the cup in his right hand to his client. "Watch out, it's hot." His oversight hit him then. "Will you need cream or sugar?"

"Black is fine." She took the cup, cradled it in both hands as if she needed the warmth more than the caffeine. "Thanks."

Spencer took his seat and prepared to launch into the details of the mission strategy he'd developed.

"When do we leave?" she asked before he'd even begun. "I don't want to wait any longer than absolutely necessary. I've wasted too much time already."

"I understand." He gulped a mouthful of coffee, ignored the burn, and braced for an argument. "I've had to make a few adjustments to our travel plans in order to avoid tipping off the enemy as to our arrival."

Those wide green eyes searched his, too much recent disappointment setting her on instant edge. "What kind of adjustments?"

"Your ex-husband is well-connected. I don't want to risk his being tipped off about our arrival." He picked up the passports he'd had made and passed them across the desk for her perusal. "In order to head off that possibility, I thought we could travel as a couple."

"Lana Anders?" She looked from the passports to him. "How did you get these pictures?"

The underlying suspicion in her voice wasn't unexpected. "You left a copy of your driver's license and the most recent photo you had of your son for your file." The guy who'd made the new passports was a true artist. The absolute best Spencer had seen. Not that he'd associated with that many forgers in the past, but a man couldn't work covert operations without rubbing shoulders with the underbelly from time to time. "The pictures were altered subtly, that's why you didn't immediately recognize them."

She stared at the passports and new driver's license for a moment or two longer. "They look authentic."

"I don't think we'll have a problem getting through the checkpoints."

Her continued hesitation had just about convinced him that she would balk at crossing this particular legal line, but then she surprised him.

"I'm glad you had the foresight to take this step." She placed the passports and license back on his desk. "You're right. He probably has me on some sort of watch list to ensure he gets a call if I show up in his country again. I should have thought of that."

He contemplated explaining to her that it was his job to weigh all the possibilities, that he'd been trained for that very purpose, but that wasn't necessary. When she'd had time to think about it, she would realize that rationale without him having to tell her. Right now he very much needed her to believe he regarded her as capable. Destroying her self-confidence any further would not be conducive to a good working relationship, a relationship he hoped wouldn't prove to be a fatal mistake for one or both of them.

"We'll be traveling on business," he went on, laying out the rest of the plan for her. "Real estate. We have a client who hired us to scout out office space in Kuwait. I've booked a hotel already. I opted for something outside the main tourist areas in order to keep our profile as low as possible."

"How soon can we leave?"

"Tomorrow morning. There's a short layover in Amsterdam, but that's actually going to tie in nicely with our cover profile. I've arranged an appointment in Amsterdam to view a commercial property. We'll need all the credibility we can manage since we don't have time to set the profiles as fully as I'd prefer."

Willow wasn't sure she understood exactly what

he meant when he said "set" the profiles, but since he was the expert on this kind of thing, she'd let him make the rules. The idea of pretending to be his wife had initially put her off, then she'd realized he was right. Definitely. That he was thinking two or more steps ahead inspired her confidence. Since this might very well be her last hope, at least until she could save up more money, she wanted the effort to be worthy.

No, what she wanted was for the effort to be successful. She wanted to escape Kuwait with her son. Once they were back in this country her attorney would take the appropriate measures to protect her and Ata from her ex-husband. Unfortunately, no matter that the American courts had ruled in her favor from the beginning, if she didn't have Ata in her custody there was nothing she could do. Extradition didn't apply to stolen children. This was the only way.

"Do you have any packing instructions?" She knew how to dress for life in Kuwait, but she didn't have any idea the fashion essentials for covert maneuvers.

"You'll need rubber-soled shoes. Sneakers will do. Dark clothing for night wear and something along the lines of khakis for daytime. Modest attire, as I'm sure you know. Our main objective is to blend in wherever we are, whatever the hour."

She got it. And he was right about the modesty thing, not that the concept would ever be a problem for her, she'd been raised far too strictly even to consider otherwise. Still, a woman in Kuwait was expected to be covered. The less skin revealed the better. Long sleeves, long hemlines, high necklines. Even though the western influence had changed the way some women opted to dress, many, especially the male hierarchy, did not approve of this choice. The only way to ensure she drew no unnecessary attention was to follow the old-school rules.

What she really wanted to know more about was this man's plan for stealing her son away from her ex and his obsessed mother. "What's your game plan once we've arrived? I mean..." She didn't want to sound dumb or impatient. The investigators she'd hired previously had kept their methods to themselves. Not asking enough questions might or might not have been a mistake, either way she didn't intend to take the risk this time. She needed to stay on top of every move. "Do you already have an idea of how you want to approach my son?"

Those gray eyes studied her for what felt like half a lifetime before he spoke. She couldn't decide if he was weighing just how much to tell her or if he simply wanted to gauge her readiness for moving forward.

"The first day we'll acclimate and do the tourist gig to make ourselves look legit. Then we'll set up surveillance and wait for the right opportunity." He lifted those massive shoulders in a noncommittal shrug. "Or we'll create an opportunity of our own."

He sounded so confident, so casual, as if he did this sort of thing every day. She wanted desperately to believe it would be so easy. But a part of her was scared to death that she would gamble on this last-ditch effort and fail, leaving her with nothing.

Not even hope.

This was the moment. Dread knotted in her chest. She'd wrestled all night with the question of whether she should tell him about the last P.I.'s investigator. She'd intended to tell Jim Colby on their first meeting and she'd actually hinted at it, but she hadn't come right out with what she knew. Part of her was scared to death this man would opt not to go through with his plan if he understood the full risk. He might see this as information he had needed before agreeing to move forward with her case and use her omission as grounds to pull out.

Anxiety tightened like a noose around her throat.

No matter how she weighed it, justified it or pretended the truth away, he deserved to know that truth. As desperately as she wanted her son home with her, she could not bring herself to allow him to go forward blind.

"There's one other thing I should probably tell you." She drew in a much-needed breath and reminded herself that she had no choice. "The last P.I. I hired, Mr. Davenport, sent a man to find my son and bring him back home to me." Willow moistened her lips and prayed that she wasn't about to make a major mistake. "He got very close. Close enough to take pictures of my baby in a number of settings and situations. I can't believe just how close he managed to get."

Those gray eyes continued to peer right through hers, as if he could see into her deepest, darkest thoughts. He asked, "Did this man learn anything that might be useful to our operation? I was under the impression none of the other investigators had accomplished anything of real value."

The realization that his deep voice contained an edge that hadn't been there before filled her with dread. If he changed his mind or decided he couldn't trust her…she just didn't know what she would do then.

"None of the others were able even to get close…except for the last one. If he discovered anything useful, Mr. Davenport didn't pass the information along to me." Don't stop now. Just do it. Say what had to be said. "Davenport did say that he had lost contact with the man he sent in—the one who got the pictures. He believes the man may have been taken prisoner or murdered by my ex-husband or a member of his personal security."

There, she'd said it.

She waited for Anders's response, her heart flailing behind her sternum so she could scarcely draw in enough air. Please don't let him back out now. Not now. They had to do this. She had to get to her baby, had to bring him home.

"This operation comes with major risks, Ms. Harris. Risks are a part of my job. But what you've just told me is all the more reason for you to stay right here while I go do what has to be done."

Relief rushed along her nerve endings, making her feel unsteady. He hadn't changed his mind about moving forward. Thank God. "I can't do that, Mr. Anders. I have to go with you. I have to help get my baby back." No risk was too great to her. She had to make him understand that.

He didn't argue the point, which surprised her. Instead, with the help of the receptionist, Connie, he took care of the necessary travel reservations. He went over a few more details with her, and then she left to return to her motel and pack. She would meet him at his office the next morning at seven for one final briefing with Mr. Colby before they headed to the airport.

Then they would get started.

She couldn't wait.

No matter what happened, she had to do all within her power to get her son back. Some part of her had the almost overwhelming feeling that if she didn't get him back now she might never see him again.

The feeling ate at her a little more each day.

She surveyed the single suitcase she'd finished packing. Several changes of clothes and the essential toiletries, nothing frivolous. She didn't dare take a picture of her son, other than the one hidden in her wallet. Even if her purse had to be searched, she felt comfortable that the picture wouldn't be discovered the way she had it hidden. Anders would carry her son's passport.

Exhausted, she plopped down on the bed next to her suitcase. She really should get some sleep. It wasn't that late. She glanced at the clock radio on the table by the bed. Nine-fifteen. But she hadn't slept well the night before and she needed to be fresh in the morning. Starting tomorrow she had to be in tip-top condition. No distractions, fatigue included. She thought about the sleeping pills the doctor had prescribed, but the hangover and dulled senses the morning after weren't worth it. She'd just have to try getting some sleep the old-fashioned way.

Shouting in the room next door made her jump. She pressed her hand to her chest and stared at the wall that separated her room from the one next door. A man's voice sounded angry, a woman's pleading. Whatever was going on, nothing about it conveyed pleasantness.

Maybe she should call the desk and complain. Like that would do any good. The desk clerks she'd encountered so far looked about as interested in their work as fence posts.

A loud crash accompanied by the sound of breaking pottery, the table lamp, she surmised, launched her into action. She'd just reached for the phone when a rap on her door paralyzed her.

It wouldn't be the people next door since she

could still hear them shouting. It was too late for someone from the Equalizers to be dropping by...wasn't it?

Standing there in the middle of the room wouldn't answer the question. She moved quietly to the door and checked the peephole.

Spencer Anders waited on the other side.

She had to admit, considering the ruckus next door, she was relieved to see him. After sliding the chain free of its catch, she opened the door.

It wasn't until she came face-to-face with him that the possibility that he'd arrived bearing bad news formulated in her sleep-deprived head.

"Have our plans changed?" She tried to steel herself for what might be coming, but there wasn't any way to adequately prepare. She wasn't sure she could handle bad news. Not now, after she'd gotten this close. She was packed, the tickets had been purchased.

"May I come in?"

In her experience when a person avoided answering a direct question then there was a problem. Her heart started to pound in anticipation of the worst.

"Sure." She managed to back up and open the door wider. "Is there a problem?"

He closed the door behind him, leaving her with nothing to hold onto. Whether it was the look on her face or the trembling that had started along her limbs, he appeared to comprehend her mounting hysteria.

"There's no problem. We're right on schedule."

She might have exhaled some of the tension just then if the ranting in the other room hadn't chosen that exact moment to explode all over again.

"Excuse me."

Spencer Anders pivoted, opened the door and walked back outside.

Confused, Willow followed as far as the door.

He turned and held up a hand for her to stop. "Stay there."

As ordered, she didn't move. Several seconds passed before she realized that she didn't have to stand here like this just because he said so. By then his banging on the door next to hers had silenced the shouting in the other room and startled her so that she couldn't think to move anyway.

What was he doing?

The neighboring door burst open. "What the hell do you want?" the man towering in the open doorway demanded.

"I'd like to speak with the lady in the room," Anders said, his tone utterly calm and oddly genial.

"She's busy right now," the lanky, mean-looking guy glaring at Anders snapped. "Unless you're a cop, I'd advise you to get lost."

Sobbing from inside the room made Willow's chest tighten.

"I'd like to do that, buddy," Anders offered, "but you see, I have a problem with jerks like you."

His next move happened so fast Willow would

have missed it entirely if she hadn't been watching so closely. He slammed the guy square in the jaw with his fist. The jerk dropped to the floor without so much as a grunt.

"You okay, ma'am?"

Willow blinked, and in that fraction of a second, Anders was attending to the woman who'd rushed past the fallen jerk and straight into her savior's arms. By the time the cops had arrived, Anders had ordered Willow back into the room and closed the door.

She peeked past the curtains and watched him comfort the woman as the police took away her boyfriend or John or whatever he was. Nearly a half hour later the cops, as well as the jerk and the woman were gone.

Willow jumped away from the window when Anders knocked on her door even though she'd watched him walk right up and rap his knuckles there.

"I apologize for keeping you waiting," he said as soon as he'd stepped back into her room.

Her brain kept telling her to say that she understood, but her lips wouldn't form the words.

That intense gray gaze settled on hers once more. "I wanted to give you one last chance to change your mind about going with me to Kuwait. I'm not sure you fully comprehend the magnitude of the danger we may very well encounter."

She should have anticipated that he would attempt to dissuade her again, but somehow she hadn't.

"I'm going, Mr. Anders. Nothing you can say will change my mind."

She stared right back at him with all the defiance she could muster in her current state of teetering between total exhaustion and absolute confusion as to what she'd just witnessed with the couple next door. Unfortunately, her body betrayed her and attempted to tremble beneath his continued visual assessment. Dammit, she should be stronger than that.

"In that case, I won't waste my time or yours." He reached for the door once more. "I'll see you in the morning, Ms. Harris. Try to get some sleep."

Then he left. No more questions or warnings, nothing. He just walked right out as if her answer had been all he needed to move forward.

Willow locked the door and slid the chain back into place. She measured how he'd stepped in to rescue the woman next door against how easily he'd accepted her answer and gone on his way.

A paradox, she decided. One she wasn't sure she possessed the wherewithal to decipher.

Whatever he was or wasn't, she sincerely hoped he could follow through with his promise to get her son back. She needed him to be able to do that.

Right or wrong, her son was all that mattered to her just now.

Call it mother's intuition, but every instinct was screaming at her that time was running out fast. Very fast.

Chapter Five

Wednesday, February 23
Aboard a flight to Kuwait

Spencer watched Willow Harris sleep. She had fought the need for hours before finally surrendering. Then she'd curled up in the window seat next to him. He was glad she'd given in. This might be her last chance to get any decent sleep until the mission was over.

Another hour and they would land at the airport in Kuwait City. He'd spent most of the travel time asking questions about the way she'd met al-Shimmari. The story went like most others with a similar ending. Girl meets boy, girl falls in love with boy. Boy uses wealth and power to take advantage of girl who has not a clue how the cultural differences will eventually impact her life.

The adage *love is blind* was too damned true.

The story got somewhat muddy during the last year she spent in Kuwait. No matter how he'd phrased the questions or from what angle he had approached the subject, she'd found a way to dodge being completely forthcoming about that timeframe.

He didn't understand her reasons for holding back. As badly as she wanted to regain custody of her son he had to assume that she would share any possible information even if only remotely relevant. That assumption would lead him to figure that nothing about that final year was significant. However, there was a strong probability that she couldn't see past the emotional wall she'd built to protect herself from those final months of her marriage. She could be holding back information that would prove useful without even knowing it. That was the part that worried him.

Of course he couldn't be certain that anything about her marriage, other than the clash of cultures, was pertinent to the current situation, but he had a feeling.

After a decade of diving into covert operations in various settings and under a wide array of conditions, he'd learned to trust his gut implicitly. His instincts had only let him down once.

Spencer leaned back deep into the seat, allowing his thoughts to wander back just over two years—something he rarely permitted. The mission had been as uncomplicated as they came, get in, retrieve the hostages and get out. He and his team had done it a hundred times before.

But that last time something had gone wrong. The

hostages were already dead when the team arrived. Spencer had taken the fall for the intelligence leak that had led to the deaths of the hostages.

He hadn't been able to prove his innocence, but neither had the military investigators assigned to the case been able to prove his guilt.

As far as he was concerned there was only one man to blame for what happened. Colonel Calvin Richards. Richards was retired now, but he'd managed to destroy Spencer's career before taking that retirement.

Bitterness burned through Spencer. This was why he didn't let himself think about that particular part of his past. His fingers tightened on the arms of his seat. He hadn't deserved that kind of end to his career. Prior to the incident two years ago he'd been touted a hero. He'd never wanted the attention that went along with being labeled a hero, but he sure as hell hadn't expected to be called a traitor.

"Would you like something to drink, sir?"

The flight attendant smiled down at him, ready to provide whatever refreshment he required. The answer to her question was no. He told himself to utter the single-syllable word but the thought of having a drink—just one—was almost overpowering. One drink would likely do the trick. He could relax…let go the tension now twisting his gut.

The other passengers seated around him in first class had been served already. Beer, wine, cocktails, bourbon. It would be so easy. Having a drink once they landed in Kuwait would be near impossible since alcohol was illegal.

Sweat beaded on his forehead. He wished he could work up the courage to just say no.

"I'll take a soda."

Willow's voice jerked his gaze in her direction. She sat up a little straighter in her seat and gazed expectantly at the flight attendant. He hadn't realized she'd awakened, much less moved.

"Nothing for you, sir?" the attendant prompted one last time.

"I'll have the same as the lady." That his voice was practically a croak made him even angrier, this time at himself for being weak as well as a fool.

"I'll be right back with your drinks." The attendant continued down the aisle.

"I can't believe I slept so long." Willow stretched her arms and torso, the motion as sleek and languid as a cat's, the soft moan accompanying those movements sounding as satisfied as a contented purr.

"You were tired." It was the only response he could dredge up from his preoccupied brain at the moment. He shifted his attention from her, careful not to focus on the alcoholic beverages being enjoyed by the other passengers, and gave himself a mental kick.

The attendant returned with their complimentary drinks. Spencer allowed the fizz of the soda to sit on his tongue before swallowing. He would not let his need to fortify himself screw up this operation. His mind was made up. The two years not withstanding, wallowing in self-pity had never been his style.

This was his opportunity to get his act together. He would not let defeat suck him in again. Willow Harris was counting on him.

Her little boy was counting on him as well, though he didn't know it yet and might not appreciate it for years to come. The next couple of days would determine the course the boy's young life took. Would he be raised as an American with his mother's influence affecting his daily life? Or would his future lie in a different world with a man who very well could be associated with terrorists?

To Spencer's way of thinking, under normal circumstances both parents should be involved with the rearing of a child. But, if there was even an iota of truth to the rumor that al-Shimmari had ties to terrorists, the man had no right to shape the life of his child.

Proving al-Shimmari's ties to illegal activities was not Spencer's job. His focus was reuniting the boy with his mother. He would, in fact, be attempting to steal the child and to smuggle him out of the country with a fake passport. If they were caught, they would face stiff penalties, including jail time.

It was common practice in these cases for one parent or the other to attempt to regain control over their child's destiny. In this case, the key was to have the child on American soil and in the care of the mother in order to claim jurisdiction for legal purposes. On his own ground, that was exactly what Willow's ex-husband had done. He, in turn, would fully anticipate that she would retaliate in kind. Unfortunately none of her previous investigators had been successful.

Spencer considered that at least one man may have died in his attempt. This gave him all the more reason to believe that al-Shimmari might not be on the up and up.

Whether he was or not made no difference to Spencer. It did, however, greatly influence the lengths the man would likely be willing to go to in order to protect his continued possession of the child. Possession was extremely important to maintaining legal custody. The American courts generally ruled in favor of the American parent. Willow had, in fact, gained a court order granting her temporary custody months ago. The Kuwaiti courts had chosen to ignore that order. No surprise there.

"I brought along a khimar to wear. I didn't know if you would think it was necessary, but I'm leaning toward that extra layer of precaution."

Spencer wrestled his attention back to the present. "I brought one as well. I planned to suggest that you wear it to ensure as much invisibility as possible." He'd hoped she wouldn't have a problem wearing the scarf. Though it wasn't necessary as a western visitor, any steps they could take to ensure she wasn't identified by anyone from al-Shimmari's circle of family, friends or business associates would be a good thing. He hadn't brought it up before in an attempt to avoid giving her anything else to worry about. He'd felt certain she would agree to the last minute suggestion.

Maybe he'd underestimated her determination to cooperate.

"Funny," she said quietly, "I never wore them before."

She didn't look at him as she said this, instead she stared out the window at the passing clouds or maybe nothing in particular.

"An act of defiance?" Was this how the marriage had started off? Or had her husband at first permitted her to cling to her western ways?

"Our relationship was different in the beginning." Her gaze shifted to the back of the seat in front of her as she spoke. "There was mutual respect. His mother didn't like that he allowed me to be American, but he seemed perfectly happy with the *me* he'd married."

"When did things change?" They'd covered some of how things started to deteriorate, but maybe if he persisted along these lines she would delve into those final months. He settled his half-empty glass on the tray and waited for her to go on with her story.

"After Ata's birth." She held her soda in both hands as if she feared a sudden bout of turbulence would catch her off guard. "It was as if he grew ashamed of me. The pressure to stay home and out of the public eye was at first subtle, but then I started to feel like a prisoner. God knows that fortress he calls a residence is more like a prison than a home."

She placed her drink on the tray above her lap, but didn't let go of the glass. "Everything about Ata became an issue. I wasn't holding him right. I wasn't feeding him properly. Half the time Khaled's mother was in charge of Ata's care. They just pushed me aside and did things their way, as if I had no say in the matter."

That couldn't have gone over very well. "How did you put a stop to that?"

For the first time since the conversation began she looked him square in the eye. "I pitched a fit. For a while things were better."

"But that didn't last long."

She shook her head. "Then my ex-husband found business to occupy my time." She leaned her head back against the seat. "To keep me away from our son as much as possible. I didn't recognize the tactic at first. I was so happy to be involved with my husband's pursuits I didn't see the hidden agenda."

This was the first he'd heard of her being involved with any of al-Shimmari's work. "What exactly did you do for the family business?"

She traced the droplets of water forming on her glass. "Since my training was in trading stocks and evaluating investment potential, he pretended to want my advice on his financial portfolio."

If Spencer had been surprised before, he was outright shocked now. Why would a man like al-Shimmari allow her access to his financial records? Sure, she'd been educated in finances, but she wasn't a seasoned pro by any means. "What do you mean he pretended to want your advice?"

She shook her head slowly from side to side. "God, I was such a fool."

Spencer didn't rush her, he just let her talk. He sensed that what she had to say next would prove key to new and vital information about al-Shimmari.

"The entire portfolio I'd evaluated for hours and hours, days really, was a hoax. What he allowed me access to was nothing more than a fake set of financial records created specifically for my entertainment."

Tension roiled through Spencer. "What tipped you off?"

"We were in his office at home. I was pointing out a problem I'd discovered when he was called out of the room for a moment. His computer screen was open to what I thought was the same data system I accessed from my own small office. So I sat down at his desk to print out a page I'd somehow failed to print. The differences in his database and the one I was permitted to access were glaringly obvious."

Spencer's tension escalated to a new level. "Did he catch you at his computer?"

She laughed, the sound dry and wholly lacking in amusement. "He didn't have to catch me. I confronted him about the differences." Another laugh choked out of her. "I was totally convinced that someone was keeping a second set of books, so to speak, in order to skim his finances. It never entered my mind that he was the guilty party."

Spencer could imagine what happened next. None of it good.

"He was furious," she went on. "He accused me of making up the data he claimed didn't exist. I was never allowed even to speak of his work or his finances again. Two months later I broached the subject of a trial separation. I'd gotten so frustrated with the way his mother kept Ata away from me and with his indifference I was ready to take drastic action." Her attention turned back to the window. "I thought maybe if I shocked him with that news that maybe he would turn back into the man I'd married. I had no idea that he'd already made plans of his own. A few days later I found myself in LAX with no ID or money."

Spencer touched her arm, the one closest to him. "Those months must have been very difficult for you." Being so far from home with no support network, surrounded by people who didn't want her, had to have been a nightmare.

She looked up at him, her green eyes filled with that haunted look that tugged at his emotions. "The hard part came when they wouldn't let me see my son again." She grabbed his shirtsleeve when he would have moved his hand away. "You have to get my son back for me, Mr. Anders. I can't keep living this way." She blinked back the tears that filled her eyes. "I dream about him, only to wake up and realize that I'm alone. Do you know how that feels? To be completely alone? So alone that nothing matters to you anymore?"

A single tear trekked down her cheek and he couldn't resist touching her again. He swiped the tear away with the pad of his thumb. No one should have to go through this kind of hell. She loved her child. She only wanted the things any mother would want. The man she'd loved and trusted had taken that away from her.

"I'll get your son back." He didn't answer the other question. "No matter what else happens, I will see that you get your son back."

The crackle of electricity between them startled him at first. But he couldn't draw his hand away from her sweet face. She needed him. No one had needed him in so long. More than that…he needed her just a little.

The sound of the flight attendant's voice over the speaker system shattered the moment. "…Seatbelts should be fastened and trays should be placed in their upright position in preparation for landing…" Another of the flight attendants hurried along the aisle to reclaim empty refreshment containers and any other trash from the passengers.

Willow kept her gaze straight ahead as the plane

started to descend. He had wanted to ask her if she'd found anything in al-Shimmari's finances that sent up a red flag for her. Obviously there was something her ex-husband had wanted to hide from her. Or maybe he just hadn't wanted her to know the true extent of his assets. But why bother to hide those? As a non-Muslim she had no rights to his holdings. If he hadn't gotten so caught up in touching her he might have asked the question.

Later, when they'd gotten to the hotel maybe he'd ask her to elaborate on what she'd found. For now, they had to concentrate on getting through customs and the airport without incident. Operations of this nature were best accomplished one step at a time.

When the plane bumped along the tarmac, Willow felt her tension start to climb once more. She'd spent the past forty-eight hours bracing for this moment and still she felt ill-prepared for what was to come.

What if Khaled learned that she was here?

What if one of his many spies saw her?

She chewed her lip and fought the panic. He wouldn't find her. Mr. Anders had taken care of a passport under an alias. She would wear the khimar. Khaled would not know she was in the country. She and Ata would be gone before he suspected she was up to anything. He surely thought he'd foiled her attempts to retrieve her son when he captured or murdered Mr. Davenport's man.

If she and Spencer succeeded, Khaled would retaliate, but she'd just have to cross that bridge when she came to it.

This was the only way.

Willow resisted the urge to look at the man next to her. There were other things she wanted to tell him. But she couldn't. She'd sworn never to tell. If she breathed a word of what she knew, Khaled would not rest until she was dead. If she were dead there was nothing she could do for Ata. His well-being was first and foremost in her mind.

Nothing else mattered.

Nothing.

Khaled's business dealings were not her problem. There were government agencies responsible for catching men like him. She couldn't be that kind of martyr. Not when her son's life hung in the balance.

She knew exactly what would happen if she told Spencer Anders or Jim Colby what she knew. They would do the same thing any of the others she'd hired would have done had they learned her secret: go straight to the FBI.

As much as she loved her country…as much as she longed to do what her brain told her was the right thing, her heart wouldn't let her do anything that would jeopardize her child's safety.

Khaled had told her what he would do if she ever told a soul. The fact that he hadn't simply killed her had been surprise enough. At first, she had been so happy that he hadn't executed her on the spot, that she had stupidly thought maybe he still loved her. But he hadn't, not the way a man was meant to love a woman in any event.

So, she'd had to muddle through alone. Her family had disowned her. She had no friends. The few she'd had before moving to Kuwait had gone on with their lives. There was no one to help her except this stranger she'd hired with the last of her savings.

She could say or do nothing that would alienate him in any way. He could never know she was keeping such a horrible secret. He was ex-military. He would not understand her reasoning.

Every step had to be carefully planned. Every word cautiously chosen.

When the seatbelt light had gone out and the flight attendant announced that they could deplane, Spencer stood and stepped back for her to exit before him. Willow dragged the khimar from her purse and wrapped it around her hair as she moved down the aisle. She had lightened her hair just a little and she'd lost some weight. She had to believe that no one would recognize her. Otherwise she might just have a nervous breakdown before they got out of the airport.

As they walked along the corridor that would take them into the terminal, Spencer moved closer, but he didn't touch her. Apparently he understood that acts of affection or touching in general were not well-perceived in this country. His apparent knowledge of the country prevented any awkwardness.

God really had been looking out for her when he'd led her to the Equalizers.

Her heart started to pound harder when they moved into the crowded terminal. She tried not to scan the crowd. She wanted to look like any other arriving visitor. If she appeared suspicious or apprehensive someone might notice.

As they approached customs, she found herself holding her breath. If they made it through this security checkpoint, they would be home free.

Several other passengers lined up in front of them.

Anders leaned down. "We'll be fine," he whispered softly.

She prayed he was right.

Working hard not to study the faces of the customs officers, she rested her gaze anywhere but on the activities going on directly in front of her.

Stay calm, she told herself over and over.

There is no reason for anyone to be suspicious. Her papers were in order. She had nothing in her possession that would raise questions.

Five more minutes and this part would be over.

One of the officers motioned for her and Anders to move forward. It was their turn.

She walked slowly up to the counter and placed her purse and small carry-on bag there. Somehow a smile tilted the corners of her mouth.

"State your business in our country."

Anders answered in spite of the fact that the man

looked at Willow when he asked the question. "We're appraising real estate for one of my clients." He smiled down at Willow before turning his attention back to the man. "And doing a little vacationing."

How could he sound so calm and cool?

The officer continued to review their passports and belongings. Willow noted nothing even remotely familiar about him. He looked to be in his forties. Medium height and weight with a bit of gray in his dark hair. His tone was brusque when he spoke, but that was typical.

Just when she'd decided she could relax marginally, the officer motioned for another man to join him at the counter. He passed Willow's passport to his associate. Her heart lunged into her throat.

The second man, who wore a similar uniform to the first, looked at Willow and said, "Madam, you will need to come with me."

Chapter Six

Willow knew what it was to be afraid. She'd been afraid many times in the past year, but not once had she been as terrified as she was at that moment.

"Is something wrong?"

She looked from the customs officer waiting for her to follow him to the man next to her who'd asked the question, his tone clearly impatient.

"Whatever the problem," Anders added firmly, "you'll need to explain it to me as well as my wife."

Willow held her breath, prayed there was merely a misunderstanding.

"There is no problem, sir," the officer assured him. "We select individuals at random for questioning. This is a security measure that is perfectly legal and of only minor inconvenience, I assure you."

Anders nodded. "Fine, but I insist on being present. Do you have a law against that?"

"No, sir. This way, please."

The wave of relief that rushed over her made

Willow sway ever so slightly. She did not want to do this alone.

Anders placed his hand at the small of her back and guided her in the direction the officer had already taken. "Don't worry," he murmured, "this won't take long."

Her entire being gravitated toward him and the protection he offered. It had been so long since anyone had protected her in any way. She hadn't realized how badly she'd needed someone to take care of her until that moment.

The interview room was small. It reminded Willow of the rooms where suspects were taken in the television cop shows. Anders sat next to her at the small table. The officer took a seat on the opposite side.

"You stated that you are in Kuwait on business." This the officer said to Anders.

"Yes," Anders responded. "I'm an international Realtor. I have a client who is interested in office space here. I've contacted a local agent." He reached into his pocket and removed a business card and offered it to the officer. "He'll be showing me a couple of spaces later this morning. I'm sure he'll be happy to verify that for you if you find it necessary to call."

It was the middle of the night. Willow didn't know who Anders's contact was, but surely he was in bed.

"Have you been to Kuwait before?"

There was no doubt as to whom this question was directed. The officer's gaze bored straight into hers.

"No." She tried to swallow the emotion tightening in her throat. "This is my first visit." Anders had instructed her on what she should say if the subject came up. She hadn't expected it to come up only minutes after her arrival in the country.

"You've been here before."

That too-familiar fear paralyzed her for two beats before the officer turned his attention to Anders.

"Have you not?" he pressed.

"Yes," Anders confirmed. "Several times."

Another uniformed man entered the room. He deposited Willow's purse and carry-on bag onto the table. He placed Anders's briefcase there as well.

The officer handed both passports to Anders. "I hope your visit is productive and enjoyable."

Willow's heart rate didn't return to normal until they had exited the terminal and picked up the rental car. As much as she wanted to close her eyes and block the memories bombarding her, she couldn't. She couldn't ignore the details of the place she had called home for three years or the incident that had just occurred, reminding her that this was not America.

"Are you okay?"

She inhaled deeply and let the breath out to clear her head. "I'm fine." It was a lie, but she didn't need him feeling sorry for her. She needed to be strong. She needed to focus on getting her son back. The memories, the fear, all of it would do nothing but distract her.

After a few miles of silence, he said, "Just so you know, that little intimidation episode back there might have had more to do with me than some random selection."

The lights of Kuwait City in the distance held her attention for a moment before she turned to the driver. "Why do you say that?"

"I'm ex-military. I was in and out of this territory dozens of times. My name might have triggered a security check."

"If you knew that was a possibility, why didn't you use an alias?" Spencer Anders appeared far too smart to make a misstep that glaringly obvious.

"I wanted them to associate you with me. Any suspicions will be on me, not you."

"Oh." Wow. Another one of his protective measures. She couldn't help being surprised all over again at having someone take steps to shelter her. "Thank you."

He didn't say more so Willow opted not to. Instead she focused on surveying the city. The lights were gorgeous, but she knew from experience that the true beauty of Kuwait City could only be seen by day. A heady mix of market bazaars and gleaming skyscrapers along a glistening coast. The mosques and souks and other sandy traces of bygone Bedouin days awaited the wanderings of tourists. No matter how much emotional stress she'd endured here she knew that beyond the glitzy opulence lay a deep sense of traditional values and warm Arabic hospitality.

She had loved this city with its diversity of people and richness of culture. It was only the man who'd brought her here that she despised. They wouldn't pass his residence en route to the hotel. Like the other wealthy residents, his massive villa lay in the Suilhibikat area closer to the heart of the city. Kuwait boasted the wealthiest population in the world; thankfully most were kind and generous people.

The situation Willow found herself in now was her own mistake. If she hadn't let love blind her four years ago she might have taken the time to consider the laws that could possibly come into play in her future. But she hadn't dreamed things would go wrong and that the child she hadn't known she would have would become a pawn in the ugly battle.

REGISTERING at the hotel at 2:00 a.m. took little time since there wasn't a line of arriving patrons. Spencer tipped the bellhop generously and closed the door behind him. When he turned around he found Willow standing in the middle of the room staring at the bed.

"There's only one bed."

True. "Remember, we're traveling as husband and wife. Our cover needs to appear realistic."

His reminder didn't erase the frown from her face, but she did seem to relax fractionally.

"It's a big bed," he added with a sweep of his hand to indicate the king-size width.

The frown eased into more of a neutral line. "It is big."

At least that was settled.

"Did you want to use the shower first?" After the long hours of travel, he was definitely ready for a shower.

She waved him off. "You go ahead. I'll…" Her shoulders lifted and fell. "…unpack a few things."

At past two in the morning he wasn't about to argue. He waited until he'd gotten inside the bathroom with the door closed before he stripped. It felt good to peel off the clothes wrinkled by too many hours sitting on a plane or in an airport.

He turned on the water and gathered the complimentary soap and shampoo and a towel before climbing beneath the hot spray. Closing his eyes, he just stood there for a couple of minutes and let his body absorb the heavenly heat.

When he'd managed to prod his brain back into action he started the cleansing routine, but a part of his mind kept going back to those tension-filled minutes at the airport.

There was every reason for Willow to be apprehensive about running into her ex-husband or someone he knew. He understood that her previous investigator had given her additional reason to believe her ex might be dangerous. But al-Shimmari hadn't killed her when he had the chance. He could have located her at any time during the past few months if harming her had been his intention. Not that Spencer was giving him any credit at all. He wasn't. The guy was on a federal watch list. He was most likely damned dangerous to the world at large, but not necessarily to any one particular individual, like his ex-wife.

Apprehension and anxiety Spencer had expected. Absolute terror he had not. The idea that being recognized had scared her that badly made him wonder if there was more she wasn't telling him. Had something happened between her and her ex that she hadn't divulged? Had she seen or heard something that gave her reason to suspect he might want to harm her if she returned?

That still didn't explain why al-Shimmari hadn't simply tracked her down and taken care of her if she had seen or heard something he didn't want her to know.

She'd been more forthcoming those last couple of hours on the plane than she had been since they'd met. Maybe she would reveal more as she came to trust that he truly was on her side. He understood that she had been let down many times before coming to him. Her trust wouldn't be easily gained. Unfortunately, time was their enemy.

When he'd pulled on fresh boxers and jeans he cleaned up after himself. He found Willow sleeping soundly on the far edge of the bed. She'd slipped off her shoes, but otherwise she was fully dressed. He pulled the cover up around her and then climbed into bed on the other side, as close to the edge as possible.

A big part of gaining her trust would include respecting her feelings. He sensed that no one had worried about her feelings in a long time. From what he could see so far, she was so accustomed to being alone that she was startled when he came to her rescue in any capacity.

No one should ever feel that alone.

He remembered what she'd said on the plane about being alone. That was the part that bothered him the most. It wasn't right. Not right at all.

He pushed away the thoughts. Ordered himself to sleep. Tomorrow, later today actually, he would need to make contact with his "real-estate" connection. There were things he needed. Things he couldn't have brought along in his luggage or in his carry-on bag.

Whether Khaled al-Shimmari was actually connected with one or more terrorist cells, whether he was capable of murder or not, Spencer had every intention of approaching this situation as if he and his security personnel were lethal as well as hostile.

Being fully armed would be his first step.

Thursday, February 24

WILLOW INHALED deeply. Her lungs filled with warm air, her senses vibrated with the scent of something earthy and delicious. She wanted to open her eyes, but that place between asleep and awake wouldn't let her go. It felt so good. She hadn't slept this well in so very long.

She snuggled deeper into the covers, hugged her pillow more closely.

Warm…smooth…hard.

Willow's mind shifted toward the awake zone. Slowly, she opened her eyes and let the room around her move into focus.

Hotel.

Kuwait.

Spencer Anders.

The sound of her breath catching echoed in the room.

"Morning."

The deep, thick sound of his voice vibrated up from his chest. She knew this because her cheek was pressed to that smooth, warm flesh. She felt the rumble.

Her initial thought was to roll away from him as quickly as possible, but his arm was around her, draped along the length of her back.

She couldn't lie here like this. What would he think?

"Good morning." She scooted away from his inviting body, noting thankfully that he lifted his arm out of her way without any awkwardness. Now if she could only unwrap herself from the cover she would make a mad dash for the bathroom.

But that wasn't going to be easy. Somehow she'd wound herself in the sheets all the way from her edge of the bed until she'd nestled against his muscled torso. The room was cool. Maybe her body had instinctively sought out the heat. And then generated a little of its own, she admittedly self-consciously.

Enough of this. She had to get up.

As if he'd picked up on her discomfort, he dropped his feet to the floor and disappeared into the bathroom. But not before she'd gotten a full view of that broad chest and those sculpted abs. Even his back looked strong and toned.

She put her hands over her face and groaned.

He had to think she was totally pathetic.

Not that she cared what he thought of her personally. She drew her hands away from her face and glared at the ceiling. None of this was personal. She had hired him to get her son back. He didn't have to like her or even respect her. He only had to do what she'd paid him to do.

If only she could maintain that sense of logic.

Kicking off the twisted covers, she managed to scramble out of bed. Her clothes were as twisted as the covers, so she righted them before sifting through her suitcase to pick out something to wear today.

Khaki slacks and a white long-sleeved pullover and sneakers.

The bathroom door opened and he emerged.

She hurried past him, careful not to make eye contact, and closed herself in the bathroom. A shower would help. She was a little off-kilter this morning. Jet lag. She just needed to regain her bearings and she'd be fine.

Truth was she hadn't woken up with a man next to her in nearly a year. Waking up next to a man to whom she wasn't married was even more unusual.

But that was her hang-up. She had plenty.

Spencer ordered room service and made a quick call to his contact. They would meet in an hour at one of the available commercial properties in the city. Touring a couple of office buildings would confirm his cover. If anyone had decided to keep an eye on him, this would back up Spencer's reasons for visiting the peaceful state of Kuwait. Meetings with a couple of random agents in the city wouldn't hurt.

When the light rap came at the door, he checked the peephole and established that it was room service. He opened the door and watched as the waiter rolled the cart into the room. He signed the check and locked the door once the waiter had gone.

The coffee smelled great. He needed caffeine. Lots of it. Though he doubted any amount of caffeine would erase the feel of Willow nestled snugly against him. The heat from her body had awakened urges he'd thought long dead. Not so, evidently. Too bad the timing was seriously off.

HE'D HAD his second cup of coffee by the time she reappeared dressed for the day.

"There's fruit and sweet rolls." Since he couldn't be sure what Willow would like, he'd gone with the safest bet. "And coffee."

She dove into the fruit before having her first cup of coffee.

Watching her eat so ravenously reminded him that she'd skipped dinner on the plane last night. He'd assumed she was too upset to eat. She was bent on making up for it now it seemed. Her lips closed around a strawberry and he couldn't help but stare.

He now knew something personal about Willow Harris the woman, not Willow Harris the ex-wife and mother. She loved strawberries. The way she closed her eyes and relished the burst of flavor on her tongue spoke volumes about just how much she loved the lush red berries.

She opened her eyes and her cheeks turned pink. "Sorry. I get a little carried away sometimes."

He sipped his coffee and tried to act nonchalantly. "I'm the same way about coffee."

She'd left her hair down. Even in the plain white pullover and khakis she looked soft and feminine, elegant somehow. Maybe it was because she was so tiny and her clothes, though conservative, fit so well.

At five-two, she couldn't weigh more than ninety pounds. And even though he recognized that her clothes weren't designer, more like bargain super center, they looked tailor-made for her figure.

Like her, he'd dressed casually. Jeans and a pullover sweater with a casual sports jacket. Though the temperature was probably in the mid-sixties, it could drop unexpectedly. Especially if it rained. No matter what the weather did, the jacket would serve another purpose as well. Weapons were illegal in this country. Carrying one required certain precautions on his part, concealment being top priority.

Willow stopped eating long enough to ask, "Did I hear you making an appointment with someone?"

He grabbed a sweet roll. "We're meeting my real-estate contact at ten-thirty. We'll look at a couple of properties today and get the lay of the land. I made a couple of other calls to local agents as well."

She poured a cup of coffee and sipped it thoughtfully before voicing her next question. "When can we drive by the house?"

She wanted a glimpse of her son. He certainly understood that. But moving too hastily could prove a mistake.

"We'll do some driving around in that area later this evening, maybe just before dark."

"Today's Thursday, the family may be out to dinner as a group tonight. Getting close to the house probably won't be difficult."

The Kuwaiti work week was generally Saturday through Wednesday. Thursday was considered a sort of family night. The next two days were holy days, not to mention a national holiday, Hala February.

"As long as we maintain an appropriate distance, I think we'll be okay," he warned, not wanting her to get her hopes up too high. Just because they drove by didn't mean she would get to see her son.

"I understand."

He wondered if she did.

She devoured another strawberry. The act made his gut clench. He had to get a handle on these unusually strong feelings of attraction and protectiveness. Certainly he intended to protect her, but he realized already that he was having difficulty maintaining objectivity.

Not good.

Recognizing the problem was the first step, he reminded himself. Just like at Alcoholics Anonymous. Not that he'd attended enough of those sessions to know what came next, but he did know that pinpointing the problem was essential in correcting it.

Funny, he realized abruptly, he hadn't thought about alcohol since that tense moment on the plane. Not that it would have done him any good. The only way to get an alcoholic drink in Kuwait was to go to a private, very illegal, party. Still, he felt some sense of relief at not waking up to the urge to pour himself a drink.

He hoped the change for the better was about getting his life back together with this career endeavor. But he had a feeling it had more to do with his distraction with his client than anything else.

And that was definitely not good. At all.

"Whenever you're ready, we'll get going." Getting his head screwed back on straight would be a hell of a lot easier outside the intimacy of this room—away from the bed they'd shared last night. No matter that nothing had happened. Waking up to her cuddled up against him had been more than enough to inspire his too-vivid imagination.

Evidently, while he'd overindulged in alcohol since exiting his military life, he'd neglected his physical needs. Now he was paying the price of having gone too long without sexual release.

She grabbed the scarf and quickly wrapped it around her head to cover her hair and neck. "Okay. I'm ready."

He shouldn't have let her come.

The realization slammed into him like an unexpected mortar round.

She was afraid. She was vulnerable. He'd allowed her to come to this country where being a woman could be a handicap under far too many circumstances.

Protecting her might very well be impossible when push came to shove.

He'd warned her about that.

Unfortunately he was the one who hadn't fully

heeded the warning, because right now he felt completely obsessed with keeping her safe. And that compulsive need jeopardized the mission overall.

All signs of objectivity had vanished the instant he'd seen the sheer terror in her eyes back at that airport.

He had no choice.

He had to keep her safe.

Or die trying.

Chapter Seven

11:00 a.m.

"You do not want to get caught on the street or anywhere else in Kuwait with these weapons."

Spencer surveyed the array of handguns his contact had to offer. A Beretta .9mm, a .40 Glock, as well as your garden variety .32s and .38s. Various ammo clips and silencers. Night-vision goggles and binoculars.

The night-vision goggles would be nice, but he was on a budget here. With that in mind, he reached for the Beretta and the .32.

His contact pushed several clips and a box of bullets across the table. "That should set you up."

Spencer paid him in cash, American currency.

"You know how to contact me if you need anything else."

Spencer tucked the Beretta in his waistband at the small of his back. The .32 he dropped into his jacket pocket. "We won't be here long enough to require anything else."

Though Patrick Bach had always been a reliable contact for most any sort of special needs any time day or night Spencer had called on him in the past, there was always risk involved in a transaction as illegal as this one. Those in the trade didn't always play by the same rules transaction after transaction. The rules changed based on the buyers and the quantity of money they were willing to spend.

Spencer had worked operations when he'd been forced to rely on his own methods for survival, including arming himself on the local black market. Bach hadn't once let him down. But there was always a first time.

As Bach packed up his wares, he glanced at Willow then he grinned and said to Spencer, "I didn't realize you'd separated from the military and gotten yourself an actual wife, Anders. I guess this is one way to keep domestic life blissful."

Spencer had instructed Willow to remain on the far side of the room and to refrain from speaking to Bach. So far she'd done so. Since he hadn't introduced her to the man, he had to assume Bach was fishing. It also meant that his arrival in-country had hit the underground grapevine. Nothing he hadn't expected.

Spencer picked up the ammo and dropped it into his pocket. "I didn't realize you'd gotten so curious about the personal lives of your customers, Bach."

Spencer didn't offer the first glimmer of amusement in response to the jab at humor.

Bach held up both hands in the universal gesture of surrender. "Just making conversation, man. Just making conversation."

Spencer leaned closer to him and smirked. "Besides, you know a guy like me never really goes back to civilian life."

A knowing grin spread across Bach's face. "Right." The devious glint in his eyes told Spencer the sly bastard had taken the comment exactly the way he'd intended.

If Bach leaked that Spencer was in-country doing illegal business related to his former career that was so much the better.

To her credit, Willow had the submissive female act down pat. Even in the elevator ride back to the lobby she stayed in Spencer's shadow. This posturing kept Bach from getting a good look at her face as they exited the building.

The fewer details he was able to pass along, in the event he was so inclined, the better. Taking every possible precaution to protect her would be in the best interests of them both.

Willow kept her gaze lowered as Anders shook hands in closure with his contact. She'd worked extra hard not to look at the man during the meeting. Even now, as she climbed into the passenger seat of the SUV Anders had rented, she didn't look up.

Once shielded behind the tinted windows of the vehicle, she surveyed Damascus Street. She could just make out the stripes of the painted water-storage tanks in the distance. Beyond that, if they were to drive in that direction, they would come upon the park and then the industrial area. She and Khaled had picnicked in that park...before. She'd never been allowed to take her son there. Khaled had rigidly dictated where and when she could take her son from the residence.

She'd wondered what he was afraid of. Asking had proven a monumental mistake. He'd lashed out at her, making her feel incompetent and untrustworthy when it came to caring for their son.

Eventually she'd learned the truth. Khaled had made so many enemies he feared their retaliation against his family, especially his only child.

Goosebumps spilled over her skin. Her son was not safe as long as he was associated with her ex-husband and his evil deeds. Somehow she had to get him out of this country. She had to find a way to ensure Khaled was never allowed custody of her child again.

Not even for a day.

On some level she felt remorse that her son would not be able to know this side of his heritage. She could try and teach him the Islamic values, but it wouldn't be the same. That was the saddest part in all this. Ensuring his safety and having him in her life equated to tearing him from the land of his birth. It was the only way.

She couldn't trust any member of her ex-husband's circle, especially not his mother. Massouma was totally fixated on every detail involving her only son's child. Once Willow took Ata away, he could never return or she would be right back at square one.

Coming to terms with that finality hadn't been easy. She'd lived in this land for three years. Her respect for these people went as deep as the oil wells that paraded through the desert beyond the suburbs of the city. But nothing or no one was as important to her as her son.

"It isn't easy being back."

Anders's comment tugged her from the depressing thoughts. The words were a statement rather than a question.

"There's a level where I feel torn," she admitted, surprised even as she said the words. "I shouldn't. I know I shouldn't. But I do."

She didn't know precisely how, but somehow he understood how she felt. Maybe because he'd spent so much time in the Middle East during his military career, or perhaps simply because he had been betrayed himself. Did he have any idea how much his appreciation for her feelings meant to her?

That he'd managed to draw her in so deeply, so quickly, was a little scary. Still, she couldn't deny enjoying the feeling of being protected.

"I'm glad Mr. Colby asked you to take this case." It was the best way she knew to thank him for his perceptiveness and compassion.

The stall in traffic allowed him to look at her for several seconds before moving forward once more. "I hope you don't change your mind before we're finished."

He held her gaze an extra beat, but the blare of horns prodded his attention back to the traffic.

Willow told herself to look away. It didn't do any good. She kept staring at his profile long after he'd looked away. She recalled the way she'd felt that morning when she'd awakened next to him. Even before that, she'd slept like the dead for the first time in months.

He made her feel safe.

It was crazy. She scarcely knew him.

That he'd separated from the military in such an egregious manner should have put her off…should have her unsettled about his trustworthiness. Yet, she trusted him completely…felt fully protected in his presence.

He had stood up for the woman, a complete stranger, in the motel room next to hers. It had been so long since she'd seen an act of chivalry so impressive and selfless that maybe she was overreacting. Then again, she hadn't had sex in more than a year. As embarrassing as that fact was, she wasn't actually ashamed of it. She'd slept with one man in college, another after settling into her job following graduation, both had been relationships versus casual sex. Her next partner after that had been her husband.

She'd never had casual sex in her life.

Part of that was a direct result of her strict upbringing. There were times when that not-particularly-pleasant upbringing had come in handy. For instance, when she'd taken up residence in Kuwait, dressing and behaving conservatively had come naturally to her. She'd been almost thankful for her parents's ironfisted child-rearing methods. But then those same methods had ingrained in her a willingness to trust the man she'd married when she shouldn't have. She'd blindly gone into that relationship and followed all his edicts without once questioning anything until it was way too late.

Not that she blamed her parents for her mess. She didn't. This was a tragedy of her own making. Still, they were not totally free of guilt here. She'd learned the hard way that lying in one's self-made *hard* bed was not the only option. Even now she could hear her father's voice echoing that sentiment, *You made your bed, you'll have to lie in it.*

The muscles in her face tightened, making her jaw clench at the old hurt. No. You didn't have to simply lie in it. There were things a woman could do, should do, when her husband mistreated her, physically or mentally.

If she'd only realized sooner what kind of man

Khaled was, she might have escaped with her son before he'd suspected her disillusionment or her plans.

That wasn't really true. If she'd suspected something wasn't right she would have gone to him and asked, assuming he had been falsely accused, just as she did when she'd discovered the discrepancy in his finances. There was no getting around the fact that she had simply been naive. And in love.

Big mistake.

Her attention shifted back to the driver, the man she respected so much despite knowing him for a period of time more accurately measured in hours than in days. Was she making the same kind of mistake all over again?

She'd watched the way he handled that illegal business with the guns. Did she really have any reason to trust him? Sure, he seemed to sympathize with her, seemed compassionate toward people in general, but did that make him a good guy deep down where it counted?

Stop it.

They were here. He was doing his job so far. She had to stop overanalyzing every single thing. She could not afford to be distracted. Her actions could very well distract him. Allowing that to happen would jeopardize what they were here to do.

Time to get her act together and focus.

Time to behave like a mature woman who had learned her lesson about trusting the wrong man. The compromise was simple. She should appreciate Spencer Anders for his seeming compassion and empathy as well as his obvious skill at doing what had to be done in this situation and environment. All the while, she most definitely should understand that his ability to get the job done did not make him a good person.

Somehow she had to learn to separate her feelings. Respect didn't necessarily have to equate to trust or…anything else. Like the feelings of attraction she had experienced lying next to him that morning.

She was a woman, she had needs. Those needs could not be permitted to get tangled up with the heat of the moment. Recognizing the problem was the key to moving forward productively.

She definitely recognized the problem. If she were really lucky, he didn't. Knowing that he knew she was even remotely attracted to him would just be too humiliating.

"Our next stop is the building on the left at the coming intersection. We're a little early." He checked his wristwatch. "Ten minutes. We'll park and wait in the car."

"Is the person you're meeting at this location an actual real-estate agent?" Anders had told her that the last guy worked on the fringes of the business as a cover for his real job—selling weapons in a country that had banned the personal ownership of weapons years ago. She had known men like that existed in

Kuwait when she'd lived here—as did those who sold alcohol illegally. There was a whole underground of illegal activities here just as there was any place else.

This was, however, the first time she'd had direct dealings with the folks who carried out those prohibited trades.

"This one's for real. I picked his agency from the listing in the local paper and called to make the appointment this morning." He parked the SUV in a narrow alley between what appeared to be two office buildings. When he'd shut off the engine he turned to her. "There's one more after this for cover purposes, and then we'll drift into tourist mode."

There was such intensity in his eyes, such determination. How could she not believe he would make this happen? She'd watched men like him in the movies, read about them in books. A hero. Every instinct told her this man was exactly that.

She had to believe.

"Oh, yeah, you mentioned that earlier."

For the first time since arriving at the airport and having that customs officer scare ten years off her life, she felt confident again.

Jim Colby had promised her.

The man he'd chosen for her case would make it happen. She believed that with all her heart.

Believing was something she was really good at most of the time. Her childhood had included a deeply entrenched certainty that without faith all was lost. She'd never once failed to have enough faith. Even when objectivity would have served her better, she'd stuck by the idea that faith would get her through whatever life tossed in her path.

Maybe that was how she'd survived when she'd feared her ex-husband might simply kill her to silence her. It would have been relatively easy in this society. Women certainly weren't the ones front and center in the mainstream. Without any other family ties here, if she'd gone missing hardly anyone would have noticed, much less asked about her.

Anders opened her door, dragging her from the disturbing speculation. She hadn't even realized he'd gotten out.

She climbed out of the SUV and followed him to the front entrance, admiring the architecture and scattered palm trees along the street as she went. There wasn't a lot of landscaping to brag about in Kuwait, but the immaculate care taken of the city was noteworthy, as was a good deal of the architecture. An art gallery across the street nudged at her curiosity. There was a time when she wouldn't have missed a gallery of any kind, even one that catered to the really bizarre alternative art she didn't particularly care for. She loved studying the work others did with their hands.

Did that make her a hands girl?

She glanced down at the right hand of the man next to her. She'd noticed his before. Nice hands. Big, but not rough-looking. Well-formed with long, blunt-tipped fingers. Not the artist type, but the capable kind made for touching a woman in ways she could only imagine.

Jerking her gaze front and center, she railed at herself for being so foolish. She'd gone off on a very inappropriate tangent there. Probably just her mind attempting to find ways to decompress. Distraction wasn't a problem, as long as she didn't obsess about any part of him she would be fine.

Right?

Right.

Okay, now she was answering herself.

Not good.

Anders signed in at the reception desk in the lobby. She waited near the cluster of chairs and potted palm trees. The ceiling soared high, allowing for a wall of windows that invited the sun to pour into the lobby. She wouldn't want the job of working the reception desk in the summer. The air conditioning might keep the room at a tolerable temperature, but there was no way to escape the harsh glare of the summer sun in this part of the world. It could be brutal.

As Anders approached her, she decided making a quick trip to the ladies' room before the real-estate agent arrived might be in order.

The sign for the restrooms as well as the elevators held a prominent position on the wall well behind and beyond the reception desk that dominated the front of the lobby.

"I'm going to the ladies' room. I'll be right back."

He glanced around the deserted lobby. "I'd feel better seeing you to the door."

There was no need to be embarrassed. He was right.

"Whatever you think is best." She headed for the designated corridor.

He stayed in step right beside her. When she reached the door, he hesitated. "Maybe I should check it out first."

"Anders, I'll be fine." She looked back in the direction they'd come. "You should wait for your appointment. You'll still be able to see this door from the waiting area."

He glanced back to confirm her assertion. "All right." That intense gaze landed back on hers. "But make it fast. I won't relax until you're back in my line of vision."

She pushed through the door, leaving him staring after her.

For a couple of moments she stood on the other side of the door wondering if he'd walked back to the waiting area or if he'd opted to hang around until she emerged once more.

She didn't remember the last time anyone had worried so about her. That he did it with such care made her feel warm inside.

Shaking her head at just how pathetic she was,

Willow moved toward the stalls. The restroom was pretty much like one found back home. The American influence in Kuwait couldn't be ignored even when it came to toilets.

When she'd relieved herself and washed up, she considered her reflection a moment. At twenty-eight she still looked young, but she felt old inside. She'd stopped feeling young and vibrant ages ago.

Willow tugged the scarf from her hair and ran her fingers through the long, blond length. She'd thought about cutting it several times, but something always got in the way. Or maybe she was afraid to change much of anything for fear her baby wouldn't recognize her.

Would he even remember her?

Pain arced sharply inside her. What would she do if he didn't? He would cry for his father…people would notice. How could they hope to get through customs and back on a plane if her child screamed the entire time?

What if attempting to steal him was a mistake?

Willow closed her eyes and fought back the emotions churning wildly inside her.

She was doing the right thing.

She knew it. She believed it with her whole heart.

Faith. Where was her faith?

Anders was waiting for her. The real-estate agent might have arrived already. She shouldn't be in here worrying about an issue that hadn't come up yet.

Taking extra care, she wrapped the khimar around her hair and neck. A few blond strands peeked past the scarf, a vivid contrast to the black silk. Her cheeks were flushed and her lips red from biting and licking them repeatedly. She needed Chap Stick.

No, what she needed was to relax.

Stay calm.

Get this done.

Summoning her wayward courage she moved to the door and pulled it open. Anders still waited near the potted palms and seating area. Evidently the other man hadn't arrived yet.

With a deep breath she emerged into the lobby and headed straight for Anders. He watched her from the moment she stepped beyond the door. That he continued to look directly at her when she stopped in front of him made her a little giddy.

Dumb. So dumb.

What was wrong with her?

She was going way overboard with this whole big-strong-protector thing. Yes, he was supposed to protect her, but that was his job. It wasn't like he was doing it because he was attracted to her or had some vested personal interest in her. Other than the case.

"He should be here any minute now."

The moment felt oddly awkward. "Good."

He looked away then, as if he felt the awkwardness too.

She stared at the floor, the plants, pretty much anything but him. Then she busied herself watching the man behind the reception desk answer the phone.

No matter that she wasn't looking at Anders. No matter that he probably wasn't even looking at her, she could feel him. It wasn't that general awareness of someone's presence…this was a pull of some sort. A feeling of nearness that overwhelmed all else.

She closed her eyes and fought the vertigo effect the unexpected sensations had on her. Jet lag, she told herself. Her emotions were oversensitive. That was all it could be. Sleep deprivation played tricks on one's mind. She knew this firsthand.

There was no reason to let this silly reaction get out of hand. She opened her eyes and surveyed the lobby in every direction except the one in which he stood. She wished the real estate man would hurry.

"You seem nervous."

The deep, husky quality of his voice shouldn't have made her shiver, but it did. Dammit.

Frustration surged. "I'm fine." She flashed him a glance that relayed that frustration. "I just want this part over with."

"I understand."

The empathy in his eyes backed up his words.

Why did he have to do that? She needed him to be that unyielding, distant man she'd met that first night.

"How could you?"

He flinched as if the words had stung somehow.

She refused to feel bad about it.

"You're right. I can't imagine how this must feel."

Why hadn't he stopped at *You're right?*

Movement at the front entrance dragged her attention there in hopes that the real-estate agent had arrived and they could get past this strained moment.

"Is that him?" she asked, hoping to avert his focus from her.

Anders turned to look at the man who'd walked up to the reception desk.

She watched as well. Something about the way the man signed the guest registry was vaguely and strangely familiar to her.

Willow stared hard at the man as he placed the pen on the desk and chatted with the clerk. The way he handled his briefcase...his mannerisms as he spoke... Somehow she recognized his body language.

She studied his profile as he produced identification for the clerk as Anders had been required to do. Then he withdrew a cell phone from his jacket pocket as if he'd received a call. He turned his back briefly to take the call.

The way the man moved...the profile...

"Oh, God."

Anders wheeled toward her, searched her face. "What's wrong?"

Fear exploded in her chest.

Impossible.

She had to be wrong.

But she wasn't.

"I know that man."

Chapter Eight

Spencer knew his first moment of sheer panic.

It was a wholly unfamiliar sensation.

He kicked it aside.

"Go back into the ladies' room." He looked directly into her eyes, noted the terror there, refused to let it affect him. "I'll make excuses for you. Stay there until I come back for you."

She didn't answer. Didn't move.

"Do you understand?"

The stridently muttered demand appeared to snap her into action.

"Okay."

She headed for the ladies' room without a backward glance or a second's hesitation.

Spencer shifted his attention to the man who had just picked up his briefcase and turned to head in his direction.

In an instant Spencer had cleared his mind of all else and stepped into character. He started forward, outstretched his hand at just the right moment to meet the other man's. "Spencer Anders."

"Yuri Avnery."

Spencer gave Avnery's hand a firm shake. "I'm looking forward to seeing the space. The location is excellent. Exactly what my client is looking for."

Avnery nodded. "Very good." He gestured toward the bank of elevators. "Shall we?"

Spencer relaxed marginally. "How long has the space been on the market?"

Avnery provided a few details regarding the previous business tenant. Spencer put on an attentive face, but his mind was on Willow and whether or not leaving her alone in the ladies' room was a good move.

Not that he'd had a choice.

When they'd boarded the elevator, Avnery asked, "Your wife decided not to accompany you after all?"

Spencer's alert status moved back into the red zone. Avnery knew the answer to that question. He'd assuredly seen Willow standing near Spencer, not to mention her name had been on the register.

"I'm afraid my wife got bored and decided to visit the gallery across the street."

He recognized that the man had in all likelihood noted her hasty retreat to the ladies' room. That shouldn't actually set off any warning bells.

Spencer hoped like hell he'd only gotten a look at her back. Even a glimpse of her profile might eventually trigger some kind of recollection if, in fact, Willow did know him.

Damn.

There were hundreds of real-estate agents in this city. How the hell had he managed to select one she'd run into before? If he believed in karma, he'd be worried. But there was no reason to believe there was a problem just yet.

"That's too bad," Avnery said. "I was looking forward to meeting her."

The interest in his eyes was undeniable. Maybe a little too interested.

"It's not often," he added, "that my clients bring along their wives for input."

Definitely too much interest. Spencer's instincts went on point. "I'm sure my wife would love to think that she had some say in the matter, but I'm afraid she's here for the shopping and sightseeing."

Avnery nodded, a smirk hovering just beneath his perfectly composed professional veneer. "I find that the female perspective is not often conducive to constructive business."

Spencer would just bet he did. Men like Avnery considered women good for nothing more than sexual and domestic slavery. He was reasonably sure this guy was Israeli. Maybe he'd been raised in Kuwait or Saudi Arabia. Whatever the case, his perspective on how women should be treated was definitely skewed.

That was the thing about men like Avnery, they

needed a female in submission to feel more like a man. He didn't have to know this guy personally to understand that his feelings had nothing to do with religion or tradition.

He could only assume that if Willow knew this man he was somehow associated with al-Shimmari, which explained everything about his attitude. He would also assume for the moment that his interest in Spencer's companion was more related to his warped view of women than the possibility that he'd somehow recognized Willow.

Avnery gave Spencer the grand tour of the suite of offices that made up the third floor of the building. He pretended to be impressed. But mostly he was worried about the woman hiding in the restroom downstairs.

He was supposed to protect Willow Harris.

They'd barely arrived in-country and already he'd made a strategic error.

Maybe all the booze had stolen his edge.

The idea that Willow might have to pay the price for his two-year layover in hell twisted like concertina wire in his gut.

WILLOW WORKED hard to slow her breathing.

She'd almost lost control there for a minute.

How did she know that man?

She'd definitely met him before. The way he moved. That harsh profile, long, wide nose...jutting chin.

Think!

Okay, calm down.

Pushing off the bathroom door, she started to pace in front of the line of stalls.

Black hair. Maybe five-eight or nine. Medium build.

She rubbed at her forehead as if that would help. It didn't. The familiarity was there. She knew him. But how?

If she knew his name…maybe that would help her remember.

Willow stopped in mid-step. Surely his name would trigger the right synapse.

Before reason had kicked in she'd made it to the door.

Anders had told her to stay in here until he came back for her.

But what if he was in danger?

What if this was a setup?

Khaled might have found out she was here with Anders and sent that man in place of the real estate man they were supposed to meet. No, that couldn't be right. Anders had contacted this guy. Hadn't he?

This was ridiculous!

She couldn't hide in this restroom like this.

Going out there and getting this guy's name was the right thing to do. Then she would know for sure. She refused to be a coward.

Willow pulled the door open before she could change her mind. The lobby remained empty. The typical workweek ran from Sunday through Wednesday, there wouldn't be that much business going on today.

That was to her benefit.

Taking care to restrain her stride, she made the nerve-wracking journey to the reception desk. The man behind the counter looked up, but he didn't ask if he could help her.

"My husband is viewing the suite of offices on the third floor. I thought I might visit the gallery across the street."

The man stared, didn't even blink.

Keep going. "Would you mind taking a message for my husband so he knows where I am when he comes down?"

"One moment."

While he rounded up a pen and paper, she covertly read the final two names on the register. Spencer Anders. Yuri Avnery.

The name didn't ring a bell.

"At the gallery across the street?" the clerk confirmed.

She nodded. "I'll be waiting there."

"I will see that he receives your message."

Willow thanked him and turned to face the front entrance. It wasn't like she could *not* go now. She'd told the clerk she was going. It had been the only way she could think of to get a look at the register. Maybe if she'd had time to plan an excuse she would have come up with something better.

It didn't matter now. She had to go.

Anders would probably yell at her.

But keeping their cover intact was too important to screw it up with a misstep this trivial.

She could do this.

It wasn't a big deal.

All she had to do was walk out the door and across the street. There was little traffic on the street and even fewer pedestrians. The chances of running into anyone she knew from before were about the same as winning the lottery.

Maybe a little less than that, but the basic concept was the same.

Concentrating on making her decision happen, she put one foot in front of the other. No looking back. No hesitating. Just do it.

She exited the building and didn't stop until she'd reached the street. When the unexpected surge in traffic passed, she crossed the street.

It wasn't until she'd gotten inside the door of the gallery that she could breathe again.

Thank God.

The shop owner glanced up at the tinkle of the bell and announced, *"Aa-salaam-aleikum!"* Peace be with you.

"Aleikum salaam," popped out of her mouth before she'd considered the repercussions of responding at all. Would the typical American tourist know to say this traditional Muslim greeting? Possibly. It

was on the Internet. Everything was on the Internet these days.

Besides, she'd said it. There was no taking it back now.

Stop being paranoid, she railed silently. She hadn't been here in nearly a year. She had never been in this gallery. Kuwait was a bustling city. It wasn't like she had to worry about running into someone from her past life around every corner. She hadn't even known that many people.

She might not even know the man with Anders right now. Anxiety and panic could be playing tricks with her mind.

So she did what all Americans were famous for doing when traveling, she browsed and made all kinds of comments to herself as well as the shop owner and she even gasped from time to time at the lovely artwork. Willow felt certain the man was rolling his eyes behind her back.

Paintings, sculpture, pottery. She studied each piece in painstaking detail, anything to keep her mind focused on something other than the man across the street.

Eventually his name intruded.

Yuri Avnery.

She called his image to mind. What precisely was so familiar about him?

The way he moved for sure.

His whole profile? She couldn't be sure.

Try harder.

Still nothing specific bobbed to the surface of that murky lake of memories. Maybe she'd suppressed so much of that past that she'd lost some details.

But she did know him, she decided after further consideration.

She was almost positive.

The bell over the door jingled and her head came up. Tension roared through her with the force of a freight train barreling down its track. She peeked around the piece she currently studied.

Three women, garbed in traditional Islamic dress, full *hijab,* whispered among each other as they hurried over to the wall where the oil paintings were displayed.

Willow let a whoosh of tension rush past her lips. She really did need to get a grip here. If she walked around acting like this someone would notice. Calling attention to herself was not the thing to do.

Okay. If she couldn't remember the guy she should start a process of elimination. First, she resurrected the long-buried images of the household staff along with the names of each man in her husband's domestic employ.

Nope. He hadn't been someone she'd run into in the house on a regular basis. Not that she'd actually thought he was. She would surely have remembered someone she saw every day.

She thought of the people she saw from time to time at the various shops she'd frequented. Not the grocery clerk. Not the postman. Not the drycleaner. Not at the pediatrician's office.

Then she moved on to her husband's business associates. Not that she saw any of them that often, but she did on rare occasions. Those would be far harder to recall.

The trio of women moved to the metal sculptures next. The gaze of the one who appeared to be the leader of the group abruptly bumped into Willow's. Willow smiled before she could suppress the impulse. The other woman quickly looked away.

God, she had to remember the rules of etiquette. No staring. No prolonged direct eye contact. No smiling.

No…

Yuri Avnery's profile suddenly loomed in her head. Only it wasn't the image she'd captured in the lobby across the street. He wore white robes…not the business suit he'd been wearing as he'd signed in fifteen or twenty minutes ago. Long white robes and the headdress, the *ghutra*. A shimmery gold over-cloak had embellished the pure white.

There were a lot of people at the event she recalled, all dressed in the very finest traditional garb. Tables. Waiters. Her husband…

Her breath evaporated in her lungs.

Oh, God.

She remembered him. Only his name hadn't been Yuri Avnery…Abdulatif something. She couldn't remember the last name.

He was her ex-husband's hatchet man. She'd only met him that once, but she remembered Khaled referring to him in just that way. She had assumed he'd meant that he was the man who got rid of the excess in his businesses. You know, the kind of man who came in and cut the fat...job layoffs, pink slips. Stuff like that.

But her husband hadn't meant that at all. Khaled had laughed at her later when she'd suggested as much.

The moment replayed over and over in her mind. The way her husband had looked at the man...the way he'd laughed when he made the statement about what the man did for him.

He was a hatchet man all right, but he didn't cut excess employees...he got rid of problems.

Like Spencer Anders.

Willow was at the front window of the gallery before she'd realized she'd moved.

She stared up at the third floor of the office building across the street.

If she was right...God, she prayed she wasn't...the man up there with Anders was an assassin.

"DOES THIS suite of offices satisfy your needs then?"

Spencer followed Avnery along the corridor that led back to the third-floor lobby that served the suite of offices.

"I have another location to preview this afternoon, but this is very much in line with my client's interests."

Avnery paused at the wall of windows that overlooked the street. "Quite a pleasant view," he suggested with a wave of his arm.

Spencer took his time strolling over to join him. So far the meeting had gone off without a glitch. Still, Willow had been certain she knew this man. It wasn't impossible that she knew him in his capacity as a real-estate agent. Her ex-husband might have sought his expertise at one time or another. Or perhaps they'd met at a social function. No matter, Spencer's instincts were nagging at him.

Something about this man was not right.

"I may want to come back and take some digital shots of the place," Spencer commented. "Unless you have photos or maybe a virtual tour on your Web site." He watched the man carefully now that he wasn't following him around from room to room. At one time he'd been particularly good at spotting a liar. "Your secretary mentioned a Web site." He hadn't actually spoken to this man when he'd made the call this morning.

Avnery nodded. "Of course. I believe you'll find everything there that your client requires."

His response was slightly stilted…the least bit hesitant. Spencer's tension escalated to the next level. "Can you spell out any unusual legalities involved with an American tenant?"

Avnery glanced down at the street. "Ah-ha. Your lovely wife appears to have grown bored with the gallery as well."

Spencer's attention rocketed to the gallery across the street. Willow stood in the floor-to-ceiling plate glass window staring up at this building…it felt almost as if she were looking directly at him.

"I am confident she won't be bored for long."

A long white limousine lurched to a stop in front of the gallery.

Spencer went for his weapon.

"Don't move, Mr. Anders. I would most assuredly dislike having to kill you here. I'm certain the carpet would be ruined and my friend Avnery would be upset with me."

Spencer turned slowly to face the imposter. The silenced end of a .9mm Ruger was aimed directly at his chest. His fingers itched to go for his own weapon.

"I am quite the excellent shot. You might want to consider that before you make a move for your weapon."

Spencer raised his hands in the air. "I'll take your word for that, Avnery."

The other man smirked. "I'm certain you know my name is not Avnery, but that is most irrelevant. Let's move to the elevator, Mr. Anders. Your next appointment will be your last, I'm afraid, but it is a command performance."

"Then let's not keep the man waiting." Spencer executed an about-face, giving his back to the man with the gun. That was, clearly, his only choice. And maybe if he kept him off guard he wouldn't remember to check to see if Spencer was armed.

"One moment, Mr. Anders."

No such luck. Spencer stopped.

Oh, well, that left him with only one option.

Avnery or whoever the hell he was patted his left side first since it was his left hand that was free. It was in the pivotal instant when he switched his weapon from his right hand to his left that Spencer made his move.

He twisted one-eighty, slammed against the man's right shoulder with his full body weight.

The silencer hissed. A pop followed.

Spencer shoved the man's left arm upward as they went down together.

They hit the floor.

Another hiss and pop.

Spencer had a good thirty pounds and six inches of height on the guy, but the other man was strong.

Enough with this.

Spencer drew back and jammed the heel of his right hand beneath the guy's chin. His head snapped upward. A final hiss and pop erupted from the weapon clenched in his hand. A violent twist of his head and the fight was over.

Spencer scrambled to his feet and ran for the stairwell.

He buttoned his jacket on the way down. Ran a hand through his hair to ensure he didn't look as if he'd just been in a fight. No need to tip off the clerk any sooner than necessary.

At the door to the lobby, he paused long enough to catch his breath. He opened the door a crack and scanned the area.

Two men hustled through the front entrance and spoke in Arabic to the man behind the desk. Spencer didn't catch everything that was said, but he got that they were looking for him.

If those men were from the limo, he had to assume that the vehicle was still out there and that meant Willow would still be close by as well.

When the two men headed for the elevator, Spencer opened the door a little wider to watch them board.

The elevator doors glided closed. He counted to three and exited the stairwell.

Barely suppressing the need to break into a run, he strode across the lobby.

"Mr. Anders!"

Spencer ignored the clerk.

He didn't have to look back to know the man would attempt to contact the men headed to the third floor.

They'd have to catch him if they wanted him.

He burst out onto the sidewalk.

Two things were immediately clear: the limo was still parked in front of the gallery and Willow was no longer standing at the shop window.

He ignored the blaring horns as he dashed across the street.

The limo windows were too dark to see inside, but the driver's seat beyond the windshield was empty.

That meant that any other occupants besides the ones who'd gone after him were likely inside the gallery.

Withdrawing the Beretta, he burst through the shop door. It wasn't like they couldn't see him coming. But he couldn't *not* go in…Willow was in there.

Other than the whoosh of the door closing behind him the shop appeared dead silent.

No signs of a struggle.

No milling customers.

Nothing.

He moved deeper into the gallery, around sculptures, beyond complicated displays of smaller pieces of artwork comprised of various mediums.

As he moved past the counter, a muzzle rammed into the back of his head.

"Mr. Anders."

Spencer froze. He analyzed the voice. Male. Western…almost.

"I've been waiting for you."

Three more men stepped out of the shadows of the farthest recesses of the gallery, weapons trained on one target…Spencer.

The man who'd spoken moved in closer behind Spencer. "Before you die," he said, his words uttered softly now as if he were speaking for Spencer's ears only, "I have only one question."

He jammed the barrel of his weapon harder into Spencer's skull. "Where is my wife?"

Chapter Nine

He'd found them.

Willow's heart sank a little more as she watched Khaled and his men force Spencer Anders into the waiting limousine. Someone from the airport or the hotel had to have tipped him off, had to have been monitoring Anders's calls from the hotel.

The vehicle pulled away from the curb. Two black cars, windows heavily tinted, moved into place, one in front of the limo, the other behind it. Her ex-husband's security detail.

She shivered.

Her next thought made her sinking heart shudder painfully.

Spencer Anders was as good as dead.

"Where would you go?"

Willow sucked in an anxious breath and wrestled her attention from the caravan disappearing in the distance to the woman speaking to her.

"Where would you go?" the woman repeated.

Three sets of eyes watched her from above dark veils, anticipating her answer. Though she didn't know their names, nor they hers, all in the car understood what had just happened.

What did she do now? She was unarmed. It wasn't as if she could try to stop Khaled and his men.

Jim Colby.

She needed Jim Colby.

Willow looked directly at the driver, infusing her expression with all the hope she could summon. "If you would be kind enough to take me back to my hotel, I would appreciate it." Willow gave the name of the hotel where she and Anders had spent the night. Her things were there and the telephone in the room would allow her to call the United States.

The woman behind the wheel, the one who appeared to be the leader of the group, nodded and turned her attention forward. The others watched in silence as their friend merged into the growing traffic.

Willow understood what they were all thinking. Her presence in this car could get them arrested…or worse.

The woman driving, the most outspoken of the group and the one who'd taken charge at that pivotal moment, had more than likely saved Willow's life.

She blinked back the tears that burned in her eyes.

When she'd realized who the man pretending to be a real-estate agent actually was, she'd rushed to the front of the shop. She'd seen Khaled's limo coming…she had known he was coming for her.

Since the shop owner had been preoccupied with a customer, Willow had gone for her only option: the rear entrance of the gallery.

The three women she'd noticed entering the shop a few minutes earlier had watched her flight. One of the women, the one driving now, had followed Willow outside and offered her assistance.

For the first five or so seconds Willow hadn't been sure what she should do. She'd almost been afraid to trust these strangers. But desperation had driven her. Anders would die and the hope of ever seeing her son again was fading fast.

She'd had no choice.

Moving as quickly as they dared without drawing unnecessary attention, the women had led her down the back alley for a considerable distance. Then they had slipped between two buildings and moved back to the street well beyond where the limo and its entourage were parked. Surrounding her in a wall of black, the women ushered Willow to the car. They'd stayed out of view there until Khaled and his men had driven away.

Willow couldn't be sure why these women had decided to help her, but she was immensely grateful.

Keeping low in the backseat, she couldn't help turning to look from time to time to ensure they weren't being followed.

"No one is following," the driver said, evidently noting Willow's furtive glances out the rear window.

Willow told herself to relax. She wouldn't be able to think rationally if she didn't calm down.

Slow, deep breaths.

Jim Colby would know what to do.

But could he do anything in time to save Anders?

Willow's chest tightened.

Probably not.

This was her fault. Her desperation was already responsible for one missing investigator. She should have stopped when Davenport had warned her of his suspicions about his missing investigator.

But her heart just wouldn't allow her to let go of the hope that she would get her baby back.

The name of the street they had just passed snapped Willow back to the present. Wait. This wasn't right. The driver had missed the turn for the hotel.

A new rush of worry ascended upon her.

What if these women weren't helping her…what if they were taking her to her ex-husband's home? There were rewards for people who showed extraordinary respect for the rich and powerful.

Stop.

Don't jump to conclusions right away. There could be a logical reason for choosing a different route than the one Willow knew. Right now she had every reason to believe these women were helping her. With that in mind she waited until they reached the next intersection to see if the driver was simply taking a different route.

Definitely not.

"We've passed the hotel," she said aloud, trying hard not to sound accusatory or nervous.

"The authorities may be looking for you." The driver glanced in the rearview mirror as she said this. "You should be properly prepared."

The woman sitting next to Willow in the backseat touched her arm. "You look like an American."

The realization that she wore a white blouse and khaki slacks bulldozed its way into Willow's awareness.

The women were right.

She would be easy to spot dressed like this. The man posing as the real-estate agent and the clerk at the desk of the building they had visited had probably given descriptions of her attire. Why hadn't she thought of that?

Willow placed her hand on that of the woman next to her. "Thank you." She met the driver's gaze in the rearview mirror then. "I don't know why you're taking this risk, but I'm sincerely grateful."

"If we do not help each other, then who will help us?" the driver said bluntly.

Truer words had never been spoken.

Obviously things were changing in this intensely male-dominated society. Slowly, very slowly, but they were happening.

The home they visited briefly belonged to the driver. Willow learned that the three women had been best friends since childhood. They used every opportunity to encourage other women to stand up for themselves as well as others in order to facilitate change.

Food and drink were offered, but Willow couldn't accept the hospitality since every minute she wasted might be Anders's last. Not to mention that the longer she stayed in the company of these generous ladies, the more risk she brought to them.

Once at the hotel Willow said good-bye to the good Samaritans who had rescued her from certain death. With their help she was now clothed in full traditional dress, from black veil to long black *abaya* and no-nonsense black shoes. She'd pinned her shoulder-length blond hair back as tightly as possible to ensure no telling strands slipped loose.

Careful to scan the hotel lobby as she went, she moved toward the bank of elevators. Half a dozen arriving guests were crowded around the check-in desk. Two others had moved on to the elevators.

Despite being fully camouflaged, Willow found herself holding her breath as she waited for one of the elevator cars to arrive. She kept her gaze appropriately lowered so as not to make accidental contact with the other guests standing close by. There were so many rules for public conduct…failure to adhere to even one would attract attention.

The elevator doors slid open, offering entrance and sending a surge of relief gushing through her. She followed the other guests into the waiting elevator car and then selected the floor above the one where her room was located. Since she had no way of knowing what might be waiting for her at the room registered to Mr. and Mrs. Spencer Anders, she needed to take precautions.

The floor she'd selected was the first stop. She emerged from the elevator and moved down the corridor toward the stairwell exit, thankful that she didn't run into any other guests.

At the exit to the stairs, she listened a moment in an attempt to hear anyone in the stairwell. Sounded quiet. She pushed through the door and listened again. Still quiet. Moving as noiselessly as she could, she hurried down the one flight.

Bracing for the worst, she cautiously eased the door open and peeked into the corridor. What she saw had her swiftly drawing back into the shelter of the stairwell. The urge to run quivered along her limbs.

Suppressing the flight impulse, she leaned against the wall next to the door. She had to think. Think! Forcing herself to recount the details, she analyzed what she'd seen. The door to their room stood open. Men in uniforms that she recognized as the local authorities were moving in and out of the room. She'd seen at least five in the fraction of a second that she'd dared to look.

What did she do now?

If she couldn't get to their room she couldn't call.

Sure she had her purse, but no working cell phone.

She had a small amount of cash and a credit card, but she couldn't use the credit card without having it traced right back to where she'd used it.

Going back to the airport with the return ticket in her purse wouldn't help. The moment she presented her passport she would be taken into custody. Not that leaving was actually even an option.

The bottom line was she was unarmed…and unprepared for a situation like this.

She had to call Jim Colby.

Waiting for the authorities to finish their work and clear out was out of the question. Anders would be dead well before then…if he wasn't already.

She had to do something.

If she'd asked to use the telephone in the home of the woman who had helped her escape the gallery the call might have led the authorities back to her and her friends. No way could she have done that. Acts of defiance were not tolerated, especially those carried out by women.

But she had to do something.

There had to be a way for her to do this.

If she didn't figure out something fast it would be too late.

Willow closed her eyes and fought the defeat sucking at her. She wanted so badly to get her baby back. To escape the reach of her devil of an ex-husband.

Right now it felt exactly as if she had failed already. Failed her child and herself.

Maybe it was already too late and she'd been too blind to see it.

Davenport could have been right, and she'd refused to accept it.

What if she was looking for a miracle?

And what if she wasn't going to find it?

Chicago
Friday, February 25, 8:15 a.m.

"CONNIE, have you heard anything from Anders?" Jim hesitated in front of his receptionist's desk. "He was supposed to call with an update last night."

Connie looked up over the rim of her coffee mug. "Technically, I don't start to work until eight-thirty, but the answer to your question is no."

She promptly returned her attention to the newspaper.

Jim wondered if she thought her prickly attitude would keep the world around her at a distance. The MO was classic. Don't let anyone close and you won't lose your focus and you damned sure won't get hurt, betrayed or otherwise screwed.

There was a thing or two he could tell the lady about keeping the world at a distance, but that would have to wait. At the moment he had bigger problems to deal with, like where the hell his associate was and just how much trouble he might be in.

When a guy was halfway around the world in a

country that didn't necessarily play by the same rules as his home base, and he went missing, the best course of action was to call an expert.

Jim knew only one man who could reach out and touch just about anybody, just about anywhere.

Lucas Camp.

"Put Anders through if he calls," he said to his quirky receptionist.

Connie glanced at her watch. "Yeah, okay."

As Jim started up the stairs, she called after him, "Don't forget you've got that new guy, Sam Johnson, coming in at nine."

Surprised that she would bother to remind him without him specifically asking her to do so, Jim tossed her a thank-you and decided that maybe she would grasp the concept of teamwork after all.

He double-timed it up the stairs and put in a call to Lucas. If he was in town he would be at the Colby Agency with Victoria by now.

Mildred, Victoria's secretary, patched him straight through to Lucas.

"What can I do for you, Jim?" Lucas asked in lieu of a greeting. "Victoria had an early staff meeting, but I'm manning her office."

Jim smiled at how this powerful man catered to the woman he loved. "Actually it's you I want to talk to." He grabbed a pen and pad in case he needed to take down any names or numbers.

"Shoot."

"I sent Spencer Anders on his first case and there may be a problem."

A brief hesitation preceded, "He's had a rough go with the bottle. We discussed that issue if you'll recall. I was sure he wouldn't let you down."

The depth of disappointment in Lucas's voice gave away just how badly he wanted things to work out for Spencer Anders.

"No, it's not that kind of problem," Jim assured. "I'm concerned I may have underestimated the need for a two-man team on this one."

"I see." The sound of movement rasped across the line as if Lucas were gathering pad and pen as well. "Give me the details." The disappointment had morphed into brutal determination. No one messed with Lucas Camp or his people.

Jim quickly explained the child-custody battle between Willow Harris and her ex-husband. "When Anders didn't call in last night I knew he'd run into trouble."

"I have a couple of contacts in the area I can reach out to," Lucas offered. "Let me make some calls and I'll get back to you."

"Thanks, Lucas."

Jim asked the other man to say hello to his mother for him, then he dropped the handset back into its cradle. Had he made a mistake sending Anders on a case like this as a first assignment? He could have gone himself, but he didn't have the geographical or cultural experience necessary to consider himself the best man for the job.

Spencer Anders had the experience.

He also had some hefty baggage. Jim would have recognized Anders's love affair with things eighty-proof or better even had Lucas not warned him. Jim noted the signs with the same ease as a well-trained physician observing the symptoms of an everyday illness.

But he'd also comprehended that Spencer Anders had the courage and grit necessary to set all else aside in order to accomplish his mission. Jim had done that himself many times in the past.

No. It wasn't Anders's preoccupation with booze that worried Jim right now, it was his enemy—Khaled al-Shimmari.

Jim's intercom buzzed and he picked up, hoping like hell it would be Connie informing him that Anders was on the line. "Yeah."

"Sam Johnson is here. I sent him up."

Not Anders, but an appointment he definitely looked forward to. "Thanks, Connie." Jim hung up the phone and stood as his appointment arrived at his door.

"Jim Colby." Jim extended his hand as Johnson reached his desk.

Johnson gave Jim's hand one quick but firm shake. "Sam Johnson."

"I'm glad you've decided to join the Equalizers."

Jim gestured to the chair on the other side of his desk, before settling into his own.

Sam Johnson was a forensics scientist by training even if he was currently employed as an orderly at a local hospital. He'd grown up, gotten educated and worked in Los Angeles County until one year ago. Like Jim and the rest of the new staff at the Equalizers, things had abruptly changed for Johnson and his life hadn't been the same since.

His visitor glanced around Jim's office. "Looks like you're getting settled."

Jim had visited Johnson at the hospital, but this was Sam's first time at the office. The way-over-qualified orderly had read the ad in the classifieds and called to inquire, but then he hadn't shown up for his initial interview. After doing some research on the guy Jim had decided to take the necessary initiative.

Jim surveyed his office as Johnson had. At least the boxes had been unpacked and discarded. More organizing would come later. "We're getting there."

Johnson's gaze met his once more, the hesitation there impossible to miss. "You mentioned two other associates."

Jim nodded. "Spencer Anders, former military, and Renee Vaughn, former district attorney. I'll introduce you to Vaughn after we've had a chance to talk, but Anders is out of the country on a case."

"I'm gonna say this right up front." Johnson leaned forward slightly, all signs of hesitation gone from his expression. "I come with major issues attached. You might live to regret your decision."

Jim relaxed more fully into his chair in hopes of setting the other man at ease. "I'm aware that there were rumors related to your resignation from your position at L.A.'s premier crime-scene investigation unit."

Unlike most employers, Jim wasn't hung up on the past. If a candidate had the right training and a desire to get the job done, that was what counted. Coming onboard with the Equalizers was a fresh start, a clean slate. History was just that, *history*.

"The case is cold, but it isn't closed," Johnson warned. "There are a couple of homicide detectives who will always be convinced I executed those scumbags. I can't guarantee they might not dig up some new evidence and decide to reopen the investigation and show up at your door one of these days. The potential to get ugly is there. You should know that."

"Let's get one thing straight." Jim propped his forearms on his desk and leaned forward to match the other man's stance. "Three lowlifes brutally and repeatedly raped then murdered your fiancée right in front of you. Personally, I don't care how they died. They got what they deserved. If you took the law into your own hands, then that's between you and whoever you pray to when times get tough. This position is yours if you want it. We start our business relationship today, no looking back, no questions about the past."

Johnson's gaze held his in a long, blatant moment of assessment. "Forgive my bluntness, Mr. Colby. But you're either a very gullible man or you were misinformed as to the manner of death in the three homicides for which I am still the only person of interest. In fact, there's some question as to the sanity of a man who would commit such heinous crimes, cloaked in vengeance or not." He drew in a deep breath. "If you need some time to reconsider your offer I won't be offended or even surprised."

Jim felt his lips spread into an outright grin. The reaction was still a little startling. "Johnson, I'm beginning to wonder if you really want this position."

The glimpse of desperation in the other man's eyes before he banished it was answer enough. "I'm here," he said, his tone trenchant, "because I want the position. I just want to make sure you understand what you're getting in the deal."

"Then we don't have a problem, Johnson, because I can assure you that you haven't done *anything* that would surprise me." He turned on the intimidation factor in his gaze to underscore what he was about to say. "And I can guarantee you that some of the things I've done would scare the hell out of you and your two detective friends out in L.A."

Jim wasn't sure whether Sam Johnson was relieved or startled, either way, the man didn't offer any more protests against his employment. With that hurdle out of the way, Jim showed him to his office on the first floor.

Only one other office remained once Johnson was settled, but Jim wouldn't fill that one right away. He hoped, at some point when their daughter was older, that his wife would come to work with him, if only for a few hours a week.

He missed her now that he worked away from home.

He needed her close…if only for a little while each workday.

Jim returned to his own office on the second floor and stared out the front window that overlooked the park across the street. Life was definitely harder for some people than it was others. Too many people didn't understand that concept, resulting in far too many negative labels.

Every single person he had hired had been labeled, maybe wrongly, maybe not. Traitor, hacker, murderer, incompetent…none of which was any better or worse than the labels he'd amassed. The question was, did these individuals get tossed away for their mistakes, real or imagined, or offered a second chance to rise above the challenges fate had thrown at them? And he wasn't talking about some conditional opportunity based on whether or not they measured up to somebody's idealistic image of good or bad.

No, not at all.

The only condition of employment at the Equalizers was very simple—can you get the job done?

Jim's vision was the same when it came to the kinds of cases he intended to take. He wanted the ones no one else would touch. Not easy, not glamorous, *desperate*.

He wanted to be the place people came when they had nowhere else to go.

That was the job he wanted to do.

No, not wanted, *needed*.

The thought ushered his attention back to this morning's primary problem.

Where the hell was Spencer Anders?

If he'd gotten himself killed already, Jim was going to be seriously disappointed. He'd expected the guy to last longer than twenty-four hours.

The real worry, though, was Willow Harris. If Anders was in trouble, where did that leave Willow and her child?

Chapter Ten

Kuwait
8:26 p.m.

Spencer lay on a cold hard floor.

As hard as the stone floor was, the coolness felt good against his aching muscles.

He wasn't sure where the hell he was right now. He'd awakened to this darkness, and so far he hadn't been able to work up the nerve to move.

Moving was going to hurt.

Bad.

They'd ripped off his shirt to make sure he felt the full impact of the torture. First they'd used him for a punching bag and then had come the electric shock treatments. His failure to cave as expected at that point was when his new friends had gotten really annoyed.

He'd refused to give them what they wanted. Eventually he'd lost consciousness.

He could imagine that a cloud of disappointment

had descended around that time. No one trained in the art of torture wanted to report to his superior that he'd failed. Oh, yeah, Spencer would wager that the lack of results had gone over like a lead balloon. He wished he could have seen that part.

But his body had had enough and subsequently had shut down. His military training had included all the techniques for enduring and suppressing the natural responses to torture tactics.

The fact that al-Shimmari had no idea where Willow was had kept Spencer motivated during the torture.

She'd gotten away.

He didn't know how, but she had evidently recognized the danger quickly enough to get out of the gallery before her ex-husband's men descended upon her position.

However, there were two obvious problems with the current scenario. One, he couldn't be sure how long she would last on her own before al-Shimmari got his hands on her. Two, she was no closer to getting her child back.

Spencer had to escape.

If he'd been more on top of his game he would have thought of that earlier.

A laugh choked past his busted lip.

All he had to do was get up and he'd get that done. Yeah, right.

Spencer rolled onto his side and held his breath

until the agony associated with moving diminished. When he could breathe again he pushed up on all fours.

This slow, painful process continued until he was upright. They'd taken his shoes, he realized as the cold of the stone pervaded the bottom of his bare feet.

No shoes, no shirt. He couldn't exactly wander the streets dressed like this.

He'd worry about that when he got out of here.

Since it was pitch-dark in here, his first step would be to determine where the door was and if there was a window. He flattened his palms on the wall and started the methodical search around the room.

He discovered the door on the second wall he inspected. It felt warmer than the floor. Wood, he decided. Traditional door handle. He moved on to the next two walls.

No window. Not that he'd actually expected one. Locking him in here with a possible escape route would have been far too stupid of his captors.

There would be at least one guard outside the door. Spencer's continued containment would not be left to chance. He doubted that they planned to keep him for the long term. However long he'd been lying here unconscious was likely a mere break to give him time to pull it together before another torture session.

He knew the routine.

The process would be repeated until one of three things happened. He broke and gave up Willow's location—which he didn't actually have—some of al-Shimmari's' men captured Willow, or until he died.

None of the above options worked for Spencer.

If Willow had managed to evade capture until now, he needed to see that she continued to stay free. Only one scenario for accomplishing that…get the hell out of here and find her.

Spencer leaned close to the door and listened for any sound on the other side.

Voices…at least two…slowly became more distinct.

Someone was coming.

He backed away from the door.

A muffled conversation outside the room kept his attention for the next thirty seconds or so. The men were discussing the need to move the prisoner.

No…not move. Get rid of the prisoner.

His Arabic was a little rusty.

The metal on metal clink of the lock disengaging sent tension rippling through him. The urge for fight or flight erupted in his gut.

He relaxed his muscles, loosened his fingers from the fists they had formed.

The best action right now was no action. He couldn't presume a line of defense until he evaluated the enemy. The one thing he could count on was that any act of aggression on his part would be met with lethal force at this point. They'd obviously decided they'd gotten all they were going to get from him.

Or they'd captured Willow.

Fury burned deep inside him. If that was the case, his priority would be to get her out of here.

An overhead light hummed to life. Spencer blinked to adjust his vision. The same kind of peephole installed in exterior doors and used for identifying visitors had been added to the only access to the room. Whoever was on the other side of the door would be evaluating the threat he represented. He worked hard to look vulnerable. Shoulders slumped, head down.

The door opened. “Against the wall!”

Spencer backed into the wall. Careful to keep his head lowered, he eyed the man who’d entered the room. One of his torture-wielding buddies. Mid-thirties. Medium build. A coward without a gun in his hand.

But he did have a gun. And there were others still outside, one, possibly two. Probably the same three stooges who’d worked him over before. Cowards or not, the odds were stacked against him.

“You are not such a lucky man, Mr. Anders.” The long white *dishdasha* that fell to his ankles like a robe and the traditional headdress just didn’t mesh with the sinister glare in his dark eyes. He strode straight up to Spencer and surveyed his face as if he wanted to remember every detail. He made a tsking sound. “Not so lucky at all.”

Spencer told himself not to respond, but he’d always had a stubborn streak. He lifted his gaze to meet the other man’s. “How’s that?”

"If you had been lucky you would have died the first time we stopped your heart. But you refused to die." Smiling, he lifted the gun so that he could press the muzzle to Spencer's forehead. "I'm afraid we have no more time for games. My friends believe you have nothing more to share, but I suspect differently. Where is the woman?"

"I told you, I don't know."

The cold steel bored deeper into his skull. "One last chance, Mr. Anders. Where is she?"

"It's a rush, you know."

Those black, beady eyes sparked with fury. "What is this you speak of?"

Spencer allowed one corner of his mouth to hitch upward. "The blast of adrenaline when your heart starts to beat again. You suck in that life-saving breath of air and—*bam!*—the heart bucks back into motion. It's like a drug, the euphoria overwhelms all else for about ten seconds."

"There will be no euphoria this time, Mr. Anders."

"You know what? You're right."

"Yes, I am—"

Before the man could finish his statement, Spencer slammed the heel of his hand into his throat.

Twisting away from the gun a split second before it discharged, Spencer lost his balance. The blast from the weapon echoed in the room, drowning out the sound of his grunt as he slammed into the hard floor.

Spencer grabbed the man's weapon and rolled to

face the door just in time to take down the next guy who burst into the room.

That left one more.

Spencer scrambled to his feet and flattened against the wall next to the door to wait for enemy number three to make an appearance.

The quickly diminishing sound of hurried footsteps told him the third guy had gone for back-up.

Bracing for battle, Spencer slipped through the open door. The larger room beyond was clear.

There were two corridors leading out of the adjoining room, as well as a staircase leading to a higher floor. Since he couldn't be sure which of the corridors the last man had taken, he opted for the stairs.

His senses on point, he moved up the stairs. As he reached the landing of the next floor, he heard the scramble of footsteps and the frantic voices below.

The cavalry had arrived.

He surveyed the hall that ran east and west of the landing he'd reached. Doors lined either side of the corridor in both directions. All closed. A massive window claimed the wall space on the landing. Spencer moved to the window and looked out over the parking area and portico that dominated the front of the grand villa belonging to the al-Shimmari family.

A half dozen vehicles lined the elegant parking area including the limo that had brought him here.

The shouted orders below signaled that the search had begun.

They would expect him to make a run for it.

That was exactly what he wanted them to think.

He chose the west end of the hall and moved to the first door on his left. He listened at the door for a few seconds before opening it. A bathroom. Not exactly a prime hiding place.

The pounding in his chest accelerated as the noise downstairs cranked up another notch.

He reached for the next door, this one on the right.

Time ran out on him just then.

The thud of footsteps on the main stairs at the other end of the hall warned he was about to have company.

Spencer opened the second door and went inside without looking or hesitating first. No time to worry about what lay on the other side.

He flinched as the latch clicked into place.

Doors flew open and banged against walls at the other end of the hall. Time to find a hiding place or climb out a window.

Spencer turned to take in the room he'd entered and came to a dead stall.

Bedroom.

A child's bedroom.

His gaze settled on the sleeping form in the middle of the small bed.

The dim glow from the table lamp next to the bed provided enough illumination for him to recognize the boy's dark hair.

Willow Harris's son.

The din in the hall jerked his attention toward the door. He had to hide.

The lever on the door moved.

Too late.

Spencer stepped behind the door at the same instant that it opened.

A man entered the room, his breath heaving in and out of his lungs as if he'd run two or three miles before bounding up the stairs. He walked around the room, opened then closed the closet door. Eventually he took care to move quietly back into the hall, closing the bedroom door behind him.

Spencer resisted the need to release a sigh of relief.

Not yet.

The exchange that took place in the hall right outside the child's room filled Spencer with dread and left him with extremely limited options.

Though the boy's room was deemed clear, one of the men was ordered to stand guard outside the room. Spencer recognized the voice of the man who gave the order.

Khaled al-Shimmari.

The door abruptly opened once more.

Spencer held his breath all over again.

He couldn't see a damned thing save for the door in his face but he could hear. Someone walked across the room, paused a moment, then crossed back to the door. Spencer turned his head toward the crack where the hinges of the door attached to the jamb.

A glimpse of the man who exited the room told him that Khaled al-Shimmari himself had entered the room to check on his sleeping child.

The door closed.

Another man was ordered to remain at the door, bringing the count to two.

It was the oldest trick in the book on Spencer's part. Hide in the last place the enemy would expect. Too bad he couldn't take credit for the strategy.

He'd stumbled upon the boy's room and gotten trapped here. Either God didn't trust him to get this done on his own or he was one lucky SOB.

Now, if he was really lucky, the kid wouldn't wake up anytime soon.

Spencer shoved the weapon into the waistband of his trousers. The bright side to this was he'd come to Kuwait to find the boy and here he was.

The not-so-bright side was the fact that they were stuck in this room.

Sweat beaded on his forehead. It had been a while since he'd had to hatch up an escape plan from an inescapable situation. The question of whether or not he could still do it weighed heavily on his mind.

For the first time since he'd made a move to give his friends downstairs the slip his body reminded him that he'd been seriously abused tonight.

He shuddered at the memory of his heart being brought to a stop at least twice and then jolted back into action, before he'd passed out. His trousers were still a little damp from where they'd hosed him down before starting the shock treatments.

He hated that crap.

Shaking off the distracting thoughts, he moved quietly across the spacious room to the window to get a look at what lay outside.

To his surprise the window wasn't a window. French doors opened onto a balcony or terrace that overlooked the lavish and well-lit pool below.

Spencer shook his head. A pool in the middle of the desert. The al-Shimmaris had it all. Too bad the family patriarch had sullied the family name with his nasty business dealings.

Khaled's father had died four years ago. As the only son, Khaled had taken over the family. Seemed strange to Spencer now that he'd married so quickly after his father's death.

Unless creating an heir was the point.

Maybe he'd never intended to keep Willow as a wife. Marrying a non-Muslim woman certainly ensured that he didn't have to worry about sharing the family wealth…or the custody of his only child.

Willow Harris might very well have been set up from the beginning.

The perfect egg donor and surrogate for a single heir.

Spencer cleared the thoughts from his head. He had to figure out a way to get out of here. Obsessing over what had or hadn't happened between Willow and her ex would splinter his attention.

He looked back at the child sleeping soundly in his bed.

Getting out of here with the boy might be impossible, but he had nothing to lose by trying.

Except his life and if he didn't succeed in getting out of here he'd lose that anyway.

Spencer eased back to the door that connected the room to the hall and listened. The search of the second floor had apparently been completed. His enemy probably presumed that he'd made a run for it, which meant they would be searching the grounds as well as the rest of the house more thoroughly.

He moved back to the double doors leading to the balcony and peeked past the edge of the curtain. That it was dark outside would prove useful once he got off the property. The way the property was lit up right now it could have been broad daylight.

What he needed was clothes, preferably something to help him blend in, and then all he would require was a major distraction to facilitate his escape.

He almost laughed at that.

No big deal. Yeah, right. He'd always firmly believed in just one kind of miracle—the ones he created himself.

First things first.

Blending in.

Time to take a risk and hope like hell that no one monitoring the security system would notice that an exterior door was opened.

Spencer disengaged the lock on the handle and opened one side of the double doors. He surveyed the balcony before easing out the door. Trying to keep the lock quiet, he pulled it closed behind him.

Pressed against the stone wall next to the doors, he assessed the milling about around the pool and extensive courtyard area. All attention appeared to be focused on the search of the grounds. Al-Shimmari had himself a mini army out there from what Spencer could see.

Oh, yeah, he was definitely going to need a distraction to get out of here.

Keeping close to the wall and in the narrow shadow of the house created by the massive outdoor lighting, he sidestepped to the next set of doors. He was about to reach for what he hoped would be the entrance to another bedroom when the curtain hanging on the door shifted.

Spencer flattened against the wall.

A woman, her gray hair uncovered, peered past the drawn curtain.

He couldn't be sure if she'd been sleeping and the ruckus had disturbed her or if she'd sensed his presence outside her room.

Sweat bled from his pores as he braced for her to open the door and step out to get a better look at the business taking place below.

To his surprise the curtain fell back into place.

Spencer watched the lever on the door, expecting it to move.

But it didn't.

He relaxed marginally.

Okay. If the room to the left of the child's room was his grandmother's, maybe the one to the right was the father's.

Spencer turned his attention in that direction.

Only one way to find out.

If he remembered correctly, Willow had told him that the kid's room was on the opposite side of the house. Had his father and grandmother felt safer with him between them considering Willow's attempts to get him back?

Putting the boy in a room with access to the balcony seemed pretty shortsighted in Spencer's opinion.

Worked for him though.

One small step at a time, he eased past the boy's room and to the next set of doors. He kept his breathing slow and even, kept his back pressed next to the wall.

He listened intently for a few seconds, didn't hear anything. Time to go for it.

He reached for the lever on the door and hoped no one had retired to this room.

One fraction at a time he lowered the lever until the latch released with a click that made his muscles jerk.

At least it wasn't locked.

With painstaking slowness, he ushered the door inward. The room lay in total darkness.

Inside, he closed the door behind him, then stood

very still to let his senses filter the atmosphere for the presence of another human being.

As his eyes adjusted to the near-total darkness he could make out the various furnishings positioned around the space. The bed was empty. Good.

He started toward one of the doors in search of a closet, but the white object lying across the bed lured his attention back there. A *dishdasha*, or what looked like one. Spencer pulled it on. The robelike covering fell all the way to his feet. All he needed now were shoes.

Moving soundlessly, he found the closet and switched on the light inside. A row of shoes provided ample selection for his needs. He slid his feet, first his right, then his left, into a pair. He reached to turn out the light but then decided a head covering could be useful if he managed to get off the property. He grabbed a white *ghutra* and turned off the light.

Before heading back to the balcony, he paused at the door leading to the hall and listened long enough to pick up on any activity. Still quiet.

That wouldn't last much longer.

Soon they would come to the conclusion that he'd either gotten away or was still somewhere in the house.

He didn't want to be around if and when they came to the latter conclusion.

The only question now was whether or not he attempted to take the boy with him.

Using the child as a hostage would no doubt facilitate his escape, but he refused to go that route. Too much risk to the child.

Seconds later, dressed in his stolen garments, he returned to the balcony and made his way back to the boy's room. The child still slept soundly. Could he count on not waking him when he lifted him from that warm bed?

Spencer considered the balcony outside. At either end a massive staircase led down to the lavish courtyard with its sparkling pool.

If he timed his move just right, when the main thrust of the search moved indoors once more, he might—might—be able to get down those stairs with the child without getting shot.

Big fat if.

If the child didn't wake up. *If* the usual exterior guards were distracted by the search. *If* the grandmother didn't decide to come outside.

Spencer stared down at the sleeping child. Could he take that chance?

Could he not? He might not be able to get this close again.

The sudden urge for a drink slammed into him full-throttle. He shook with the force of it.

Just one drink. If he could have just one he might get through this.

His hands started to shake hard. His breathing grew ragged. One drink would give him the edge he needed.

Otherwise he couldn't hope to succeed.

He knew his limits. Hell, he'd spent the last two years learning what a failure he was. The very people who had depended upon him in the military considered him a traitor.

What had he been thinking taking this job? What had Jim Colby been thinking? Spencer was a has-been. He had no right pretending he could do this anymore.

Shouting in the hall outside the room jerked his gaze toward the door.

The search was resuming full force...*inside* the house.

Time was up.

He had to move now or lose any possible window of opportunity.

But could he do it?

Fury at his own weakness hardened inside him. One thing was certain, he damn sure couldn't do it standing around here feeling sorry for himself.

Spencer opened the door onto the balcony and took a quick look. Still clear.

Determination surged. This was the reason he'd come to Kuwait. Willow Harris was counting on him. He would not let her down.

He threw back the covers and scooped the sleeping child into his arms. The slight feel of the child's weight made him tremble. His life was now literally in Spencer's hands.

Failure was not an option.

Spencer pivoted and moved quickly out of the room.

If he survived getting off the property, all he had to do was find Willow.

Chapter Eleven

Willow sat in the taxi.

She stared at the compound that was Khaled's home.

If she didn't do this, Spencer would die. If he wasn't dead already.

The last few hours were one huge blur of trying to find a way to get in touch with Jim Colby. When she'd finally worked up the nerve to steal a cellular phone from a tourist it had been too late. Jim Colby had been out of his office.

She'd considered going to the American Embassy or to the authorities, but either option would have been a mistake. Her ex-husband was too powerful. Not to mention that she was here via an illegal passport. The embassy would try to help, but their hands would be tied where Ata was concerned. The red tape would have gotten in the way of them helping Spencer in time. She couldn't risk that they would insist on holding her since her passport was a fake.

"This is your stop, yes?"

Willow's attention snapped to the driver. He'd waited patiently for her to make up her mind to get out. She cleared her throat. "Yes." Digging into her purse she withdrew the last of her cash and handed it to the driver for the fare. "Thank you."

She reached to open the door and the man's voice stopped her. "You are sure this is where you want to get out?"

As impatient to be on his way as the man was, he obviously recognized her anxiety. She met his gaze in the rearview mirror, concern radiated from his eyes.

"Yes, this is the place."

Willow looked away before she could lose her nerve.

She got out of the taxi and closed the door.

Staring at the gate that led into the fortress, she reminded herself that her son was in there. If she got to see him just once, maybe dying wouldn't be so bad.

But then what would happen to him?

There was nothing wrong with being raised in this culture. Most of the people here were good people. It was the secrets she knew about her husband that made her fear for her child's well-being.

Men like Khaled drew hatred. Her son would always be in the line of fire. He would never be safe here.

Willow squared her shoulders and walked to the gate.

The guard, one she didn't know, on the other side stared hatefully at her through the bars. "What do you want?" He looked her up and down as if she were an object to despise.

She reached up and pulled down the dark hood of the *abaya,* revealing her blond hair. "Tell Khaled that his ex-wife is here for her son."

The guard's eyes widened. He might not recognize her but her request had certainly told him who she was. He jerked the radio off his belt and spoke quickly, too quickly for her to understand his frantic words.

Mere seconds later the gate opened and she was hauled inside.

Evidently the word that Khaled's former wife had arrived spread like wildfire. As two guards escorted her to the house, people, Khaled's personal army, seemed to line up to watch her long somber march to the house.

The massive double doors on the front of the house stood open. Khaled waited just inside, his dark gaze burning into her even from a dozen yards away.

As she was ushered across the threshold, her ex-husband shouted an order for his army to resume its search, then he turned that furious expression toward her. "You know where to take her," he said to the guards.

Willow's heart butted against her sternum.

She would not get to see her son. The disappointment dragged her heart to her feet. How could the man she'd once thought she loved be so cruel?

The guards took her to Khaled's private office. She

was left inside alone, but she wouldn't be really alone. The guards would remain stationed outside the door.

The flare of something like a flashlight past the windows and door leading into the courtyard snagged her attention. What in the world was going on out there?

She walked to the window and pushed the curtain aside. People swarmed like bees. All the exterior lights were on and numerous large, handheld lights were being used to search for something.

The idea that she might be able to escape into that mayhem had no sooner crossed her mind than the guard taking up a position outside the French doors captured her attention.

She should have known that her former husband would cover that avenue as well. She'd tried to run away too many times in the past. He knew all her tricks.

The sound of the door opening behind her drew her around to face the man to whom she had once been married.

"You are a fool." He ground out the words as if speaking to her left a bitter taste on his tongue.

She folded her arms over her chest and took a couple of steps in his direction. "It isn't the first time I've been a fool."

Fury flashed in those dark eyes that used to make her swoon with just a look. "I warned you what would happen if you ever returned."

He had. And for a long time that warning had

worked. She had stayed in America, leaving the work of attempting to retrieve her child to hired professionals. But no more. Ata was her son. She had wasted too much time already. She had been wrong not to come before.

"I've come for my son," she said bluntly. No use pretending. He knew why she was here. "If you let me take him, I will keep my mouth shut." She stared straight into those cruel eyes. "If you don't, then my attorney will send a letter detailing everything I know about you to the American government."

Her threat fell on deaf ears. Khaled laughed so hard he lost his breath. Fear snaked around her chest and squeezed until her lungs felt ready to explode.

When he'd stopped laughing, he glared at her. "I am not afraid of your attorney or your government. I gave you the opportunity to live because you are the mother to my son. I did not want to have to one day tell my son that killing his mother had been necessary." He took a step in her direction. She held her ground. "All you had to do was stay away. But you could not. You kept sending your hirelings. And now here you are, threatening me. How dare you!"

She refused to surrender to the fear. "I want to see my son." Surely he wouldn't deny her that. Whether he allowed her to walk out of here again or not, surely basic human compassion would force him to honor her request.

"No." He took two more steps, bringing him directly into her personal space. To her credit, she didn't flinch. "You have left me no choice. You will die just like your friend."

Oh, God. She was too late. Anders was dead. Hurt ripped at her heart. She had done this…she had cost him his life.

Desperation seared through her veins. She lifted her eyes to his and clutched at one final straw. "I know you love me, Khaled. Otherwise you would have killed me when I discovered some of your secrets. You let me live because you loved me. You still love me." She searched his eyes in hopes of finding a single glimmer of compassion. Maybe it wouldn't work but it was worth a try.

"Yes," he admitted softly. "I do love you. But not enough," he added cruelly.

The door burst open and Khaled wheeled around to face the intrusion. "What is it?"

The guard looked terrified.

Willow sidestepped her ex to get a better look at the other man.

"Did you find him?" Khaled demanded.

Find him? Willow stared up at her ex and realization dawned. He was talking about Anders. He had to be. Hope bloomed in her chest. Maybe he wasn't dead. *Please, God, don't let him be dead.*

The guard's shoulders slumped even further. "No, we did not find him. He has disappeared."

"Then what do you want?" The demand was a vicious roar.

"It is your son, sir."

Terror gripped Willow's heart.

"What about my son?" Khaled grabbed her by the arm as if he suspected whatever he was about to hear was somehow her doing.

"He…he is missing."

SPENCER LEANED AGAINST the back of the small house and caught his breath.

Lady Luck had to be shining on him big-time. He'd thought for sure he would be nailed trying to get the boy out of the compound. Instead, he'd encountered practically no resistance.

He'd made it down to the courtyard, then hesitated behind a clump of palm trees to get his bearings. The men searching the property for him had all moved to the front of the house for some reason. Damned strange.

Never one to look a gift horse in the mouth, he'd headed for the back of the property since the front was clearly out of the question. He'd found a smaller gate with only one guard. Perfect.

The guard had been preoccupied with determining what was going on up front. He hadn't seen or heard Spencer coming.

One well-placed blow and the guy was down for the count.

Once he'd escaped the compound, the next obstacle had been staying out of sight on the street. People would notice a man running with a child in his arms.

He'd had to weave around and between residences, staying in the shadows as much as possible.

The strategy had worked…so far.

He needed a telephone. Since Willow was still out there somewhere he had to assume she would attempt to contact the office. If Spencer were damned lucky a single phone call would complete this mission.

The boy had roused once. Evidently the darkness and the *ghutra* had prevented him from seeing Spencer's face. The child had squirmed around for a bit then he'd nestled against Spencer's chest as if he'd felt right at home.

Knowing it shouldn't have been that easy, Spencer had racked his brain for an answer. Then he'd known. The *dishdasha* he'd taken from Khaled's room had apparently been worn before. It had been on the bed. Maybe it was a sleeping garment. Whatever the case, the other man's scent must have lingered on the garment. Since the child hadn't been able to see who was carrying him, the familiar scent must have kept him calm.

Spencer hoped that wasn't where his luck would end.

He had to have a phone.

So far, each house he'd checked had been occupied.

Except this one.

He pushed off the wall and moved to the rear entrance. He was pretty sure no one was home here. There was no car. The house was dark. He had to take the risk. He needed a phone.

There was no time to waste.

He'd checked the exterior of the home for signs of an alarm system. He'd found no indication there was one. Since both doors and all the ground-floor windows were locked, he would need to break in.

Bracing the child against his left shoulder and keeping that arm snugly around him, Spencer used a well-placed kick to force the side door open.

Two more slams against the wood were required before the door burst inward.

He stepped inside and listened beyond the sound of his own breathing.

Silence.

He was relatively certain that if anyone had been at home they couldn't have missed his entrance.

After closing the door, he went in search of a telephone. He found one in the hall. After turning on a table lamp, he entered the necessary numbers and waited for the call to go through.

It was nearly midnight, that meant about three in the afternoon in Chicago. Colby should be in his office. If he was out, Connie would just have to get him on his cell phone and do the talking for Spencer.

Spencer sat down in the closest chair. He peered down at the boy nestled against his chest. Willow had missed her child so desperately. She would be thrilled to have him in her arms again. The idea that he would be able to give that to her made Spencer feel a sense of pride and confidence he hadn't felt in a very long time.

Made him feel other things as well. Things he had no right to feel. Willow Harris sure as hell didn't need a guy like him. She was far too good for him. But that truth didn't keep him from wanting her.

Connie's voice echoed in his ears. As impatient and unfriendly as her tone was, he felt himself smile at the welcome sound.

"Connie, it's Spencer Anders. I need to speak to Jim Colby. It's urgent."

"Spencer? Is that really you? We thought you were dead. You've had us all worried sick."

Spencer heaved a sigh. "I thought I was dead too, but I'm not." His body reminded him that he might have a fractured rib and he definitely had a number of contusions and abrasions. "I'm in a hurry, Connie, patch me through to Colby."

"All right, all right. Don't be so pushy. I'm putting you through."

Spencer leaned his head against the wall behind the chair. God he was tired. But he was alive. And he had the boy. All he had to do now was find Willow and give her son to her.

"Anders, you okay?"

Jim Colby.

"Yeah. I'm okay. I escaped the al-Shimmari residence about an hour ago." He licked his lips and let the new burst of pride well in his chest. "I've got the kid."

The accolades he'd expected didn't come.

Silence echoed across the line.

Wasn't this supposed to be good news?

"We have a problem, Anders."

Damn.

Spencer tried to keep his sense of humor about him. "You mean besides the fact that we're going to need a covert extraction to get out of this country?"

"Willow called here about three hours ago. She'd managed to get her hands on a phone. We traced it back to an American tourist visiting Kuwait for the Hala festival. The guy had reported the phone stolen."

Spencer knew that the bad news was coming. "Where is she?" Dread started its ominous creep through his veins.

"I'd stepped out of the office so I didn't get to speak to her personally. But Connie did. Willow told Connie that you had been taken prisoner by al-Shimmari."

"Where was she when she called?" Panic tightened in Spencer's throat. If she'd called in three hours ago, where the hell was she now? "Did Connie tell her to stay out of sight?" If she had laid low somewhere, he could go to her now and turn her son over to her.

That thought had hope cutting through all the dread and worry.

"We don't know. She didn't say. Listen, Anders,

she was worried about you. She told Connie that she was going to find a way to help you."

The memory of all those people who were supposed to be searching for him moving to the front of the al-Shimmari property zoomed into too-vivid focus.

"Oh, hell." Spencer closed his eyes and fought the images that attempted to flash before his eyes next.

Willow had been the distraction he'd needed.

She had surrendered herself, drawing everyone's attention to her.

His eyes snapped open and he sat up straighter. "I know where she is."

"You think she's turned herself in to al-Shimmari?"

Hearing the words out loud sharpened the pain twisting inside him. "Yeah, I'm sure of it."

The soft protests of the small boy sleeping in his arms reminded Spencer that he would need more than a distraction this time. He'd need a miracle.

"Lucas Camp has contacts there," Colby said. "I've got him working on this. Give me your location and someone will come for you and the child. Let us get the two of you to safety and then we'll rescue Willow."

No way. "I'm not going anywhere without her."

"I understand how you feel, Anders, but think about how Willow would feel. She would want you to ensure her son was safe first. You know that."

As much as Spencer didn't want to admit it, Colby was right. Willow would want him to do whatever necessary to protect her son first and foremost.

"All right. Get me some backup." Spencer gave his location. "As soon as someone is here to take care of the boy, I'm going after her."

"If you go back in there before we have measures in place," Colby warned, "we might not be able to help you, Anders. You need to stand down until I give you the go-ahead."

"I'll take my chances."

Spencer hung up the phone. He didn't want to argue with his new boss. Every moment they argued was another wasted.

He needed someone here to take custody of the boy. Now.

After that, he could handle what came next.

It was Khaled al-Shimmari who needed to worry.

Chapter Twelve

Tears spilled past her lashes and joy trembled through her as Willow stood in the doorway of her son's room.

Spencer Anders had succeeded.

He had escaped with her child.

Thank God.

Khaled whirled from his son's bed and flew at her like a madman. "Where is he?"

Willow tried to hold back the smile, but she simply couldn't do it. "I have no idea."

Khaled's fingers clenched around her throat and he slammed her into the door frame. "Tell me where he has taken my son!"

She gasped for breath, but even the fear of death could not diminish her elation at knowing her son was away from his father and this family.

Khaled put his face closer to hers. "If you do not tell me the truth I will kill you now."

"I…don't..know," she managed to choke out.

"Khal!"

The hold on Willow's throat loosened ever so slightly as her ex-husband glared toward the feminine voice that had spoken. "This is none of your business, woman! Go to your room!"

Khaled's mother, Massouma, didn't back off. She would not be bossed around by her son within the walls of their home. In public perhaps, but not here. Willow remembered well just how much power the woman wielded.

"Let her go."

The cold fury in Massouma's voice made Willow shiver. As much as she appreciated the relief of having Khaled's hand fall away from her throat, Willow knew that this woman was no ally to her.

"He will not leave Kuwait," Khaled threatened, his fury burning a hole through Willow once more. "Your friend will die and so will you." His fingers clenched into fists at his sides as if to punctuate his promise.

"If you kill her now," his mother inserted coldly, "you will have no leverage with this thief who took your son." She inclined her head and stared with pure hatred in her eyes at Willow. "You can kill her later. If you had taken care of her months ago as I suggested, you would not be facing this problem now." Massouma turned more fully toward her son and tugged her dark cloak higher on her shoulders. "I am going to bed now," she announced as if the subject of murder had not been broached. "I will expect you to have resolved this matter by the time I rise."

No wonder Khaled had no heart, his mother was a monster. Willow had known the woman was cruel and obsessive, but she'd never imagined just how evil and merciless she could be. Thank God Spencer had gotten her son out of here. She did not want these evil people raising her child. They were a disgrace to their country and their faith.

Khaled grabbed Willow by the hair. "Come with me."

She struggled to keep up with his furious strides, especially when he descended the stairs. She fell more than once. Each time he jerked her upright, almost tearing the hair from her scalp.

She knew where he was taking her…to the room he used for interrogating those he presumed to be enemies.

If he got her down there…she wouldn't have a chance of escaping.

She had to think of something.

A diversion.

Anything to give herself a chance, however slim, of getting away.

"Wait."

He stopped at the bottom of the stairs. "Tell me where my son is and I will end your life quickly. No pain or suffering. You have my word."

How kind. And God knew just how much his word meant to her. "Giving you the location won't help."

He jerked her face up to his, almost snapping her neck. “Where is he?” he growled from between clenched teeth.

Willow wet her lips and prayed she would be strong enough to do this. “If the man who took Ata doesn’t see me he won’t show at all. I have to be the one to meet him. That was the deal we made.”

“This is not acceptable.”

Khaled started dragging her forward once more.

“You can be close by,” she assured him between groans of pain. “He just can’t see you. He has to believe I came alone.” Please, God, let this work.

He halted, glaring down at her once more. “Where is this meeting to take place?”

God, please don’t let him see the lie in her eyes. “First, you have to promise me that you’ll do this the way I tell you.”

“I don’t have to promise you anything!” he screamed at her, his whole body shaking with the force of it.

Willow shuddered. “Please, Khal.” She hadn’t called him by that familiar name in two years. “If you don’t listen to me, he’ll disappear and neither of us will ever see Ata again. You don’t know this man. He’s…” *Everything you’re not,* she bit back. “He’s done this before. He warned me that if I didn’t make it he would sell our son to the highest bidder to recoup the money I’m supposed to pay him.” She hated lying, but she had no choice.

For the first time since this had begun she saw fear

in her ex-husband's eyes. Of all people, he knew how vicious his enemies were. Any one of them would pay dearly to get their hands on his son.

His fingers unknotted from her hair. She stumbled before regaining her balance. "If you are lying, I will slowly, very slowly, peel every inch of skin from your body *before* I kill you."

"I'm telling the truth," she lied some more. "He's waiting for me right now. I wasn't supposed to come here like this." Might as well try to gain a few more points. She blinked rapidly, prompted her eyes to tear. "I got worried that I'd made a mistake. I decided to come here and warn you, but it was too late."

She hadn't realized until now what a good liar she'd turned into. Marrying the wrong man had forever changed the landscape of her life. If her prayers were answered, this monster would not get the chance to ruin her son's life.

"You expect me to believe that you still have feelings for me?" His disgust was answer enough as to whether or not he had any for her.

Not that she cared. She'd long ago lost any fondness for this man.

"I just want our son to be happy, Khal." This much was true. "He needs both of us."

For one fleeting instant his face softened. But the instant was gone in a heartbeat. "You will never again be his mother. You are not fit to be his mother, nor are you fit to be my wife."

She looked away to prevent him seeing the anger she felt blazing in her eyes. He was the one who wasn't fit, but now was not the time to debate that issue.

When she'd regained control and adopted a contrite expression, she urged, "Let me go to him before it's too late."

"Where?"

"Remember," she worked up the courage to say, "he can't know you and your men are there or he won't show. He has to think it's me alone."

"Where?" he demanded.

"The park where we used to picnic." He would know the one. "Near the painted water tanks off Damascus Road." At one time it had been their favorite place to go. How could she have been such a fool? She'd really thought he loved her. Now she would pay the ultimate price for her naiveté. That she could live with…as long as her son didn't have to pay for her mistakes.

Khaled manacled her arm savagely. "We will do this your way…for the moment."

She nodded her understanding.

He issued the necessary orders to his men as they exited the house. At the limo, she hesitated.

"I can't show up in your limo," she protested. "It's not that far…I could walk."

The murderous glare he pointed at her made her shiver in spite of her best efforts to appear strong.

"And let you make a run for it? I think not." He ordered one of his men to call a taxi.

She wasn't surprised that he would willingly do so. No taxi driver in the city was going to risk infuriating the al-Shimmari family. The driver would do exactly as Khaled ordered.

A few minutes later the taxi had arrived. Khaled instructed the man exactly what he was to do. He was not to allow Willow to get out of the car until she reached the park. She was not to make any calls on the driver's cellular phone. The driver was to take her straight to the park and then he was to go away and never speak of this event again.

Willow felt sorry for the poor taxi driver. He looked terrified. She could definitely relate.

Well, as long as her son was safe, she could live—or die as the case might be—with that.

As she climbed into the taxi she said a final prayer for her son and for Spencer Anders.

God speed, she beseeched. As long as they were anywhere but here they would be safe.

That really was all that mattered.

SPENCER HAD PARKED on a side street that allowed a good visual of Khaled al-Shimmari's front gate. He'd watched in confusion as those gates opened to allow a taxi entrance.

Why would a taxi be ordered at this time of night considering what was going on?

Instinct nudged at Spencer that all hell was about to break loose.

Once Lucas's people had arrived to take the boy, Spencer had laid out a strategy. He had been provided with ammo for the weapon he'd taken from the guard who'd tried to kill him. He'd been dropped off at his rented SUV with an international cell phone and any tools he might need. Spencer had easily hotwired the vehicle, but disabling the steering-lock mechanism had been a little more difficult. Nothing he hadn't done before.

Lucas's people had offered to supply him with a vehicle, but if he was caught, he didn't want al-Shimmari to know he had backup.

With the SUV usable, he'd driven here to wait. Lucas had insisted he would provide a diversion of some sort. Spencer could only guess at what he had in mind. Maybe a visit from some local government official. A command performance with a terrorist contact. Something to get al-Shimmari out of his house.

Two of Lucas's friends were out there somewhere watching and ready to step in if the need arose. Spencer sensed that the four men and one woman he'd met tonight were some sort of special ops unit, but he'd known better than to ask questions. The woman and two of the men had taken the boy to a safe place. The kid had cried once he'd awakened fully, but he would be okay. The woman appeared to know how to handle a frightened child.

The boy would definitely be a hell of a lot better off with anyone other than his heartless father.

Then had come the hard part.

Waiting.

Spencer kept thinking about how much pain Willow had endured at the hands of this lowlife scumbag. She hadn't suspected for a moment what she was getting herself into when she'd met this jerk.

He'd used her for his own purposes and then he'd gotten rid of her.

Spencer had to admit that maybe the man had cared for her on some level. After all, simply killing her when he'd shipped her back to the U.S. would have made his life a lot less complicated.

He'd had a reason for allowing her to live and since Spencer couldn't come up with any other reason, it had to be love—or some facsimile thereof. Spencer had his doubts as to whether or not the man was capable of the real thing. More likely she had been like a prized possession that he hated to lose.

"And maybe you're obsessing," he muttered.

Whatever the bastard's reasons for allowing Willow Harris to live, Spencer was glad. She deserved to be happy. She deserved to have her son back…and to be loved the right way.

That definitely left him out of the pool of candidates. He was so screwed up he couldn't be counted on for much, certainly not commitment. This job was about as committed as he could get.

Spencer scrubbed a hand over his unshaven face. Even managing to get the job done appeared to be a bit of a stretch for him.

But he refused to give up.

Willow Harris was counting on him.

Jim Colby was counting on him.

Evidently the only person not counting on him was *him*.

The gate opened once more and the taxi exited.

"What the hell?"

Spencer strained to see if there was a passenger.

Oh, yeah, there was definitely a passenger.

He couldn't tell if the passenger was male or female.

The gate closed as the taxi pulled away.

Spencer tapped his fingers on the steering wheel. Should he continue to sit here or should he follow the taxi?

Damn.

He reached for the gearshift to slide the vehicle into Drive, but movement at the gate drew his attention.

The gate yawned open once more.

Spencer gripped the steering wheel with both hands as he watched for a vehicle to exit the property.

A black SUV pulled out onto the street and headed in the same direction as the taxi.

Then the big white limo glided through the open gate.

"Bingo."

Another black SUV followed the limo from the

property. Spencer waited a few seconds before he shifted into Drive and took that same route.

Lucas's people would follow as well, he figured. Only he doubted he or al-Shimmari would see them. These people were good. Damn good.

The streets of Kuwait were quiet. Most of the homes and all of the shops he passed were dark. People were asleep in their beds with no idea that something sinister was taking place right outside their windows.

Spencer thought of that little boy he'd carried for miles tonight. He couldn't let that child down, he decided. The boy would need his mother. Somehow Spencer had to see that Willow made it through this night.

He'd never held a child like that.

Not even once. He had a couple of nieces and nephews, but he'd always been gone during family holidays. The few times he'd visited home in the past five years, the kids had stayed clear of him. His sisters had insisted they were just afraid of strangers. His sisters were probably right. Spencer had been, still was, a stranger to what was left of his family.

His folks had died a long time ago. His sisters were the only family he had left and he didn't bother to give them the time of day very often.

That was a shame.

He should have done better.

He wondered how Willow's folks would feel if

they realized what she'd been through while they were busy pretending she didn't exist. Someone should tell them that she deserved better.

Funny, he mused, how reflective a man got when he knew he was in all probability going to die.

Self-pity wasn't Spencer's style.

Better men than him had died for a lot less.

But he would be damned if he would go down without a fight.

Or without taking al-Shimmari with him.

That might just make it worthwhile.

The limo and the two SUVs took an abrupt right, but the taxi continued on.

Spencer lay back.

Did he follow the limo or the taxi?

His gut told him to stick with the taxi.

Let Lucas's people stay on the limo.

Spencer had always gone with his gut and it had only let him down that once. Even if that time had been devastating, it was hard to beat those odds.

Giving the taxi plenty of space, he followed its lead.

The driver pulled over at the park near the two massive water tanks.

Spencer parked a safe distance away.

He decided not to wait for the next move.

Ensuring the interior light was in the off position, he opened his door and eased out of the vehicle. No one had emerged from the taxi just yet.

There wasn't much in the way of streetlights in the

area. Spencer used the darkness to his full advantage. He took a position next to a cluster of palm trees.

His fingers wrapped around the butt of the weapon protruding from his waistband.

A sense of calm fell over him and he recognized it for what it was.

He was ready.

To do what had to be done…or die trying.

Chapter Thirteen

Willow scooted to the edge of the seat and prayed her words wouldn't fall on deaf ears. "Please, sir, I know you're afraid—"

"Get out of my taxi," he ordered without looking at her.

Khaled had given him strict orders. To deviate would be to sign his own death warrant. She understood why he wanted no part in this.

Still, she needed his help.

It wouldn't take Khaled long to discover that she had lied. When he realized that Spencer Anders was not coming, he would kill her.

She would do anything—anything—to protect her son but every fiber of her being resisted the idea of surrendering to certain death. She wanted to see her son again. Wanted to hold him…to watch him grow up. To be there for him.

"You must get out now," the man repeated. "I

cannot help you." As firm as his words were she heard the quiver of regret as well.

He probably had family too. She couldn't ask him to sacrifice his life...his family. "I know." But when he drove away she would be left alone with no possible help. Unwilling to give up yet, she went on, "If you could just call the authorities as you drive away and let them know that you noticed trouble in the park."

"I cannot! Please! Get out!"

"He's going to kill me," Willow pleaded. "Just call the authorities, that's all I ask."

The driver said nothing.

Willow had done all she could. He would either call the authorities or he wouldn't.

She was wasting time. If she got out now, she might have a chance at running.

As she opened her door she hesitated. "Thank you. I know you'd like to help." She couldn't hold this against the driver. This was her mess. He was an innocent bystander. She'd made the choices that got her here. Pushing him to do something that would get him or someone in his family hurt was wrong.

Willow got out of the taxi. The vehicle sped away the instant the door thudded to a close.

She drew in a deep breath and surveyed the park. She struggled to retrieve her memories of the area. Which way should she run? What was close by? There was an industrial area somewhere beyond this point. But she wasn't sure she could make it that far before she was caught.

Headlights switched on in a vehicle just down the street. The blinding glare made her feel exactly like a deer trapped in the hypnotic beam of an oncoming car.

Willow's heart surged into her throat.

Had Khaled already figured out that she was lying?

Or was this some other threat?

Panic crushing against her chest, she turned all the way around to see if his limo was coming yet.

The unknown vehicle rolled toward her.

She had to run.

Dragging in a big breath, she took off, deeper into the park.

"Willow!"

She couldn't slow down or he would catch up with her.

"Willow! Wait!"

Her brain caught up with her frantic race. She knew that voice.

Willow skidded to a stop and turned around.

Spencer?

If he was here...where was her son?

She started running again, only this time she ran toward the vehicle...toward Spencer's voice.

He met her halfway. "God, you're all right."

She didn't understand. "Where's Ata?" Surely someone else hadn't taken him. Pure terror roared through her.

"He's safe. Come on." He grabbed her hand and moved back toward the SUV. "We have to get out of here."

Willow kept looking around expecting to see Khaled pop from behind a palm tree or one of the water tanks.

Then she saw the headlights. Three sets.

"It's him." Her legs stopped moving. She couldn't take another step.

The limo and its accompanying SUVs screeched to a halt between their position and the vehicle Spencer had abandoned to come after her.

"This way!"

He ran the other way, pulling her along behind him.

"There's no place to go," she argued. Didn't he see? It was over. They had lost.

At least her son was safe.

For now…but what would happen tomorrow or the day after that?

She lagged behind the man pulling at her.

Spencer stopped abruptly. She slammed into his back.

"Listen to me." He grabbed her by the shoulders and gave her a little shake. "This isn't over. We haven't lost yet. Now stop fighting me and *run!*"

He was right, she realized with a burst of adrenaline.

The sound of doors thudding to a close behind them triggered another explosion of adrenaline deep in her chest.

She grabbed Spencer's hand and ran like hell.

A bullet whizzed past her ear and the panic rocketed once more.

Spencer took charge of the forward momentum, zigzagging to make them a more difficult target for their pursuers.

The tromping behind them grew louder. Spencer knew the enemy was gaining. He was already dragging Willow. There was no going any faster.

But he had to try. Both their lives depended upon evading the enemy for as long as possible.

To her credit, she worked hard to keep up.

There were lights in the distance. He hoped that meant houses or something they could use to put a buffer between them and the enemy.

More shots flew.

Two or more weapons, he estimated.

"They're shooting at us again," Willow cried.

Spencer wasn't so sure.

He pulled her behind the next clump of palm trees. "We need to assess what's going on back there."

Al-Shimmari and his men didn't appear to be coming any closer. Lucas's men had obviously shown up.

"What's happening?"

She was afraid. Spencer put his arm around her shoulders. She was trembling. "Sounds like Jim Colby came through with that backup we needed." He didn't take the time to explain that the help actually came from Jim's stepfather, Lucas Camp.

Willow wilted in his arms. He held her close to his chest for a moment. As much as he'd like to stay just like this for a little while longer, he recognized it might not be safe.

"We should keep moving just in case."

She wiped her eyes and nodded. "You're right."

"We'll work our way back to my SUV, taking a wide path around the trouble." The exchange of gunfire had fizzed out. He hoped that meant Lucas's men had neutralized the threat.

Recalling that Kuwait was still finding landmines from the Iraqi invasion years back, he slowed their progress, and took care where they walked.

As they reached the SUV, his instincts started to nag him. He hadn't heard any gunfire in the last couple of minutes, but he hadn't heard anything else either.

Something didn't feel right.

He opened the passenger-side door. "We should get out of here." Lucas's men could take care of themselves. His top priority had to be getting Willow to safety.

The thud of a vehicle door slamming wrenched Willow's attention toward the limo. Someone was still in the limo?

"Get in," Spencer ordered. "Get in and drive to the embassy. I'll be there soon."

"But I—"

"Do it!" He felt certain that without the sticky

politics of having her son with her, she would be well protected at the embassy.

A figure moved around to the front of the limo. Spencer leveled his weapon and took aim.

A woman.

He hesitated.

Big mistake.

The shot exploded from the woman's weapon. He felt the sting sear through his chest.

He started to squeeze off a round, but something stopped him. His fingers wouldn't obey the order his brain kept giving.

"Spencer!"

He blinked, couldn't wrap his mind around what was happening.

"Spencer, come on!"

Willow was tugging him toward the vehicle.

"Did you really expect it to be this easy?"

Willow ignored the woman. She kept pulling at Spencer, trying to get him to safety. She didn't need the aid of the moonlight or even to look to recognize the woman who had spoken.

Khaled's mother, Massouma.

"Why're you doing this?" Tears spilled down Willow's cheeks. She couldn't get Spencer to take another step. "Hurry," she murmured. "Please, Spencer."

He tried to do as she asked, but he only succeeded in falling to his knees.

She attempted to pull him back to his feet. Her hand landed on something warm and damp.

"Oh, God."

He was bleeding.

The shot had hit him in the chest. Panic showered down on her like acid rain, scalding her skin and stilling her heart.

"I knew better than to depend upon my son to take care of this situation," the cold-hearted woman said as she stopped only a few feet from where Willow huddled close to Spencer. "He has a soft spot for you that has proven his undoing." Massouma waved the gun in Willow's face. "Now, where is my grandson?"

Willow couldn't think.

Spencer was bleeding profusely.

She had to do something.

"Where is he?" Massouma demanded.

"I don't know where Ata is," she snarled at the woman who was as much a devil as her son. "If this man dies, we'll never know where he is." She added that last part in hopes the woman would call for help.

She should have known better.

"I wanted you dead months ago," the matriarch of the al-Shimmari family announced proudly. "The upcoming negotiations are far too important to risk any interference or problems. These people do not tolerate mistakes."

"Please," Willow begged. "Help me." Spencer was dying. Couldn't she see that?

"You were his only mistake. The fool fell in love with you and married you before I could stop him."

Why did Massouma keep talking about this? They were wasting time. Spencer needed help now. He was bleeding to death. His frantic gasps for breath were ripping Willow's heart right out of her chest. She had to do something.

His right hand was trapped between their thighs. Somehow he pushed against her leg with that hand.

Then she realized why.

The gun.

He still had the gun in that hand.

"You're wrong," she argued with the woman to distract her. "He never loved me. He just wanted to create an heir."

Willow slid her hand between her and Spencer and inched her fingers over the butt of the weapon as he released it.

"You think he couldn't have had his choice of women?" Khaled's mother laughed haughtily. "He wanted you. He was so stupid."

She kept saying *was*. Did she assume he was dead?

"Why don't we ask Khal?" Willow suggested as she moved her hand and the weapon forward slightly in preparation for some sort of action. God, she hoped she could do this. She'd never fired a weapon in her life.

"We cannot ask him, he's dead."

Shock radiated through Willow. "What? You can't know that. He could still be out—"

"His men went into the park, not Khal. I tried to explain to him how stupid he had been. He was jeopardizing everything, but he would not listen. So I killed him myself before he could further embarrass my husband's name. Not to worry, my dear. My grandson will be trained properly. He will never show this kind of weakness."

Spencer was dying right in front of Willow and this crazy woman just kept talking.

"We have to help this man or we'll never be able to find Ata," Willow urged, her voice pleading.

The long pause that followed sent a new wave of desperation washing over Willow. Spencer was running out of time.

"Get him to his feet and we'll take him for medical attention," Massouma instructed. "Then I will have my grandson back."

Willow didn't argue. She got to her feet and leaned toward Spencer as if she were going to pull him to his feet. Instead, she thrust out her hand, pointing the gun at Massouma.

Willow didn't hesitate. She fired.

A single moment of distraction had done the trick. Massouma's assumption that Willow intended to cooperate had been *her* undoing.

A startled expression on her face, the woman stumbled backwards. The gun in her hand fell from her useless fingers. She crumpled to the ground next to it.

The sudden silence was deafening.

A guttural sound whispered from Spencer's throat.

Willow had to stop the bleeding.

She had to do something.

Ushering him down onto his back, she placed her hand over the wound and attempted to staunch the loss of blood.

What did she do now?

Where was that backup he'd told her about?

"Please!" she screamed as loudly as she could. "I need help! Somebody help me!"

Chapter Fourteen

Saturday, February 26
9:10 a.m.
American Embassy, Kuwait

Willow couldn't stop wringing her hands together. She was exhausted and she wanted two things: to see her son and to hear news about Spencer's condition.

Spencer. She didn't even remember when she'd decided to start calling him by his first name. It had just happened naturally.

The doctors had stabilized him as best they could at Amiri Hospital, but then he'd been airlifted to a regional trauma center for surgery.

His condition had been listed as critical.

Fear flared in her chest. She had prayed and prayed that he would be okay. That she would get a chance to thank him.

She closed her eyes and let go a heavy breath. She wanted to do more than thank him. She wanted to tell him how she'd felt things for him that she had feared she would never again feel.

Right now, prayer was the only thing she could do for him.

She'd spent several hours in the custody of the authorities. They had finally released her to the embassy's representative. She'd made her statement as to the events that had taken place since her arrival in Kuwait. She was pretty sure she would still be in custody if it weren't for a man named Thomas Casey.

Casey had explained that Lucas Camp, Jim Colby's stepfather, had contacted him regarding Willow's situation. It was Casey's team of specialists who had jumped in to help her and Spencer. She remembered there were two men, but Spencer had been bleeding to death in her arms and there hadn't been time for formal introductions.

Once she'd been released by the authorities, Casey had taken her to the hotel where she and Spencer had stayed that first night. She'd showered and changed and then she'd come here.

Casey had promised that he would see that she was reunited with her son. And he'd also promised to keep her updated on Spencer's condition.

So far neither had happened.

She was trying to be patient. Food and drink had been offered, but she had no appetite. She did, however, appreciate being clean. Having her little boy see her with blood all over her would have been bad.

It was still difficult for her to believe that her ex-husband and his mother were both dead. She squeezed her eyes shut and blocked the image of her pulling that trigger. She'd never shot anyone before. She'd never even fired a weapon before.

But she'd had no choice.

If she hadn't pulled that trigger she and Spencer would both be dead right now. Her son would have ended up with that woman. Massouma had talked of some kind of negotiations with dangerous men who didn't tolerate mistakes. Willow felt certain this was why her instincts had been prodding her to act quickly to get her son back.

Willow opened her eyes. She'd done the right thing killing the woman.

No question.

A soft knock on the door drew her head up. Her breath caught at the idea that this might be Casey bringing her son to her.

She was on her feet when the door opened.

Thomas Casey entered the room. But he was alone. Disappointment sent the anticipation draining out of her.

"Where's Ata?" She held her breath, needing to hear good news.

"He's here," Casey assured her. "I wanted to speak with you a moment first."

Fear shattered inside her again. "Do you have an update on Spencer's condition?"

"He's out of surgery now and holding his own. It's

still too early to forecast a full recovery, but the doctors are optimistic."

Thank God.

Her relief trembled through her. She was so tired, she didn't know how she was still standing.

"Thank you for keeping me posted. May I see my son now?"

"Of course." Casey gestured for her to sit down. "Let's talk about your travel arrangements."

Somehow Willow managed to sit without taking her eyes off the man who appeared hesitant to tell her some portion of whatever he had to say. "Is everything okay?"

He smiled patiently. "Everything's fine."

He really did have kind eyes. For a man who looked as if he could take on the most intimidating opponent, he really was nice, with broad shoulders and a heavily muscled build. He appeared extremely fit and capable. She would never be able to thank him and his team of specialists enough.

"You haven't seen your son in over eight months, is that correct?"

Willow nodded. Worry that he'd been hurt during that time and she didn't know suddenly plagued her. "Is he okay?"

"We had a local doctor give him a thorough onceover just to be sure, and he's perfectly healthy."

Then why didn't he bring her baby to her?

"I need to make sure you understand that he may not recognize you."

The idea was one she had already considered, but hearing it out loud sent denial rushing through her. "I'm his mother. He'll recognize me."

"Of course he will, but it may take some time. I just don't want you to be alarmed if he appears afraid of you. I've been involved in a couple of reunions of this nature. I want you to be prepared."

He was right. Her son had only been sixteen months old the last time she'd seen him. For a sixteen-month-old, eight months was half his life. He might not recognize her right away.

Anguish ripped through her.

Stop it. That was selfish. She had to be patient.

This was not her son's fault. The last thing he would need with all the coming changes in his life was her overreacting.

"I understand, Mr. Casey. Thank you for helping me to brace for the possibility."

"I've made arrangements for the two of you to return to the United States on a flight this afternoon. If that's acceptable to you."

She started to object. To say that she needed to see Spencer first. But she wasn't family. If he was still in the ICU, she wouldn't be able to see him.

Right now, her son had to be her top priority.

"I appreciate that. Would someone be able to keep me posted on Spencer's condition?"

"Jim Colby will be receiving updates twice daily."

Okay, that would work. She could call Mr. Colby's office.

Casey pushed to his feet. "I'll go get your son now."

Anticipation soared. "Thank you," she offered. "Thank you for everything."

"I'm glad we could help, Ms. Harris."

Casey left the room and barely a minute later he was back with her baby in tow.

Willow worked hard at keeping her tears at bay. "Hey, sweet boy," she whispered. She'd called him sweet boy all the time…before.

Ata resisted at first, but eventually he came to her.

Careful of how tightly she hugged him, she inhaled his baby scent. He had grown so much. He was beautiful.

Her chest filled to the bursting point with joy.

She had her baby back.

No one would ever take him from her again.

She would keep him safe.

Her baby soon became fascinated with her hair. She laughed and cried in spite of her best efforts not to become too emotional.

She was alive. Her baby was alive.

And they were going home.

Monday, March 21, 10:20 a.m.
Chicago

SPENCER REVIEWED the case file for the assignment Jim Colby had just given him. It would be his first since his surgery.

It wasn't a field case, just one that required research that could be done from his desk. Spencer would be on desk duty for at least another month.

Colby wanted to ensure he was in top physical form before putting him back on field duty.

He couldn't think about his surgery or the bullet he'd taken without thinking of *her*.

Willow had called every single day to check on him, but she hadn't once asked to speak with him. He could have called her, he supposed. But he'd wanted her to make the first move…if she wanted to make a move.

That was the thing. He knew how he felt. He wanted to get to know her better. He was pretty sure she'd felt something for him. But her feelings might have been prompted by the stress of the situation or simply by the need to hang on to someone.

He just didn't know.

She wasn't that far from here. St. Louis was within driving distance. But she had her son to take care of. She was likely busy getting her life back together.

As he was, he told himself.

But he missed her.

He kept thinking of how soft her skin had felt. Of how much he'd enjoyed waking up next to her that one morning.

More than anything he wanted to make her happy.

He could do it. He was certain of that now. He'd given up the booze. Period. He'd made a number of decisions about his life. He wanted to make his position at the Equalizers one that people would be talking about instead of his past. He wanted to buy a house.

He wanted a lot of things, but mostly he wanted her in his life. And he wanted her son too.

The intercom on his desk buzzed. He picked up. "Anders."

"Spencer, there's someone here to see you. She doesn't have an appointment."

She. Hope foolishly sprouted.

"Is this about a case?" It might not be her. No point in getting all excited for nothing.

"Of course it's about a case," Connie snipped. "This is a firm that takes cases."

Spencer couldn't help smiling. Their receptionist was definitely one of a kind. "Send her on back, Connie."

He didn't question why a new client would ask to see him versus going to Colby. Maybe the boss was out this morning.

Spencer stood in preparation for meeting the client. Willow Harris appeared at his door.

She smiled and he lost his breath as well as his ability to speak. Even his knees went a little weak.

"You're looking good, Mr. Anders."

Mr. Anders. Not Spencer.

"Thank you." He didn't know how he managed the words around the huge lump in his throat, but somehow he did. "You look pretty great yourself." She did. The pale-green dress looked cool and fresh and highlighted her lovely green eyes. The hem of it fell all the way to her knees as usual, but he loved that about her. She looked…really great. "How's Ata?"

"He's doing wonderfully. It's like we were never apart." She glanced around his office as if she wasn't sure what to say next. When her gaze collided with his once more, she said, "I was in town and I wanted to drop by and thank you for what you did for me and my son."

Ah. So that was why she was here. "Thanks aren't necessary." He couldn't bring himself to say he'd only been doing his job. "Have a seat." He indicated the chair in front of his desk.

"Actually." She wet her lips; his gaze followed the movement with far too much interest. "I was hoping you could take an early lunch. I'm buying."

She looked so sweet, so sweet and so nervous.

He shouldn't read too much into her offer, but he just couldn't help himself.

"To thank me?" he suggested. The suspense was killing him. He had to know.

Her expression turned serious. "Partly." She took a big breath. "Mostly I wanted the opportunity to talk to you about where we go from here. I mean, I thought we might…have dinner or go to a movie sometime."

Obviously reading his confusion, she added, "I decided to move to Chicago. I had a job interview this morning. I got the job. I'm going to check out apartments this afternoon."

He couldn't take it anymore. "There's one still available in my building." In fact, the apartment was right across the hall from his. Jim Colby had recommended the building. "It's a great place."

"That sounds promising. So, are we on for lunch?"

Damn. He'd forgotten she asked him to lunch. "Yeah. Sure." He moved around to the front of his desk. Just standing this close made him ache with need. "But I can't let you buy."

She frowned. "Why not?"

He lifted his shoulders in a shrug. "Conflict of interest."

"But my case is closed."

He had to touch her. He reached up, slid the pad of his thumb over her soft cheek. The need to touch more of her was almost overwhelming.

"You're right," he surrendered. "You can buy…as long," he murmured, "as I get to kiss you right now."

"I thought you'd never take the hint."

He didn't want to rush this. He wanted to enjoy every nuance of looking at her…of touching her.

First he plunged his fingers into her hair. He tilted her face up to his and he got lost in those beautiful eyes. Before he could snap out of the mind-blowing trance, she tiptoed and pressed her lips to his.

The kiss was soft and sweet, and at the same time hot and needy. He wanted so much more, but that would have to wait. He intended to take his time every step of the way. No rushing. No mistakes.

She and her son deserved the absolute best he could give. He intended to start with his heart.

JIM COLBY checked his schedule. Since he had no appointments for the next couple of hours he intended to go home and have lunch with his wife. And if their daughter took her nap on time, perhaps lunch would develop into other satisfying activities.

He stood and started for his door. He hesitated at his window and watched a moment as Spencer Anders and Willow Harris crossed the street hand in hand. Jim smiled. He was glad to see those two connect. She'd called him at least twice every day to check on Spencer. It was about time the two stopped beating around the bush and got it together.

His own life was definitely coming together now. His three associates were onboard. The receptionist he had chosen was warming up to her work.

The Equalizers were off and running.

As their reputation built and word got around, business would boom.

For now, he was happy with the small cases they'd gotten. The bigger ones, like Willow Harris's, would come. He had exactly the right associates, not to mention a few handy connections, to handle anything that came their way.

The intercom buzzed. Jim turned back to his desk and pressed the speaker-phone button. "Yeah."

"Jim, there's a guy on the line who says he needs to speak with you. He said it was urgent."

"Thanks, Connie. I'll take it."

Jim pressed the button for line one and picked up the receiver. Urgent was exactly the kind of case he was prepared to take on.

He looked forward to the challenge.

Maybe this call would be the next big case that only the Equalizers could handle.

* * * * *

Dante Raintree stood with his arms crossed as he watched the woman on the monitor. The image was in black and white to better show details; color distracted the brain. He focused on her hands, watching every move she made, but what struck him most was how uncommonly *still* she was. She didn't fidget or play with her chips, or look around at the other players. She peeked once at her down card, then didn't touch it again, signaling for another hit by tapping a fingernail on the table. Just because she didn't seem to be paying attention to the other players, though, didn't mean she was as unaware as she seemed.

"What's her name?" Dante asked.

"Lorna Clay," replied his chief of security, Al Rayburn.

"At first I thought she was counting, but she doesn't pay enough attention."

"She's paying attention, all right," Dante murmured. "You just don't see her doing it." A card counter had to remember every card played. Supposedly counting cards was impossible with the number of decks used by the casinos, but there were those rare individuals who could calculate the odds even with multiple decks.

"I thought that, too," said Al. "But look at this piece of tape coming up. Someone she knows comes up to her and speaks, she looks around and starts chatting, completely misses the play of the people to her left—and doesn't look around even when the deal comes back to her, just taps that finger. And damn if she didn't win. Again."

Dante watched the tape, rewound it, watched it again. Then he watched it a third time. There had to be something he was missing, because he couldn't pick out a single giveaway.

"If she's cheating," Al said with something like respect, "she's the best I've ever seen."

"What does your gut say?"

Al scratched the side of his jaw, considering. Finally, he said, "If she isn't cheating, she's the luckiest person walking. She wins. Week in, week out, she wins. Never a huge amount, but I ran the numbers and she's into us for about five grand a week. Hell, boss, on her way out of the casino she'll stop by a slot machine, feed a dollar in and walk away with at least fifty. It's never the same machine, either. I've had her watched, I've had her followed,

I've even looked for the same faces in the casino every time she's in here, and I can't find a common denominator."

"Is she here now?"

"She came in about half an hour ago. She's playing blackjack, as usual.

"Bring her to my office," Dante said, making a swift decision. "Don't make a scene."

"Got it," said Al, turning on his heel and leaving the security center.

Dante left, too, going up to his office. His face was calm. Normally he would leave it to Al to deal with a cheater, but he was curious. How was she doing it? There were a lot of bad cheaters, a few good ones, and every so often one would come along who was the stuff of which legends were made: the cheater who didn't get caught, even when people were alert and the camera was on him—or, in this case, her.

It was possible to simply be lucky, as most people understood luck. Chance could turn a habitual loser into a big-time winner. Casinos, in fact, thrived on that hope. But luck itself wasn't habitual, and he knew that what passed for luck was often something else: cheating. And there was the other kind of luck, the kind he himself possessed, but it depended not on chance but on who and what he was. He knew it was an innate power and not Dame Fortune's erratic smile. Since power like his was rare, the odds made it likely the woman he'd been watching was merely a very clever cheat.

Her skill could provide her with a very good living, he thought, doing some swift calculations in his head. Five grand a week equaled $260,000 a year, and that was just from his casino. She probably hit them all, careful to keep the numbers relatively low so she stayed under the radar.

He wondered how long she'd been taking him, how long she'd been winning a little here, a little there, before Al noticed.

The curtains were open on the wall-to-wall window in his office, giving the impression, when one first opened the door, of stepping out onto a covered balcony. The glazed window faced west, so he could catch the sunsets. The sun was low now, the sky painted in purple and gold. At his home in the mountains, most of the windows faced east, affording him views of the sunrise. Something in him needed both the greeting and the goodbye of the sun. He'd always been drawn to sunlight, maybe because fire was his element to call, to control.

He checked his internal time: four minutes until sundown. Without checking the sunrise tables every day, he knew exactly when the sun would slide behind the mountains. He didn't own an alarm clock. He didn't need one. He was so acutely attuned to the sun's position that he had only to check within himself to know the time. As for waking at a particular time, he was one of those people who could tell himself to wake at a certain time, and he did. That talent had nothing to do with being Raintree, so he didn't have to hide it; a lot of perfectly ordinary people had the same ability.

He had other talents and abilities, however, that did require careful shielding. The long days of summer instilled in him an almost sexual high, when he could feel contained power buzzing just beneath his skin. He had to be doubly careful not to cause candles to leap into flame just by his presence, or to start wildfires with a glance in the dry-as-tinder brush. He loved Reno; he didn't want to burn it down. He just felt so damn *alive* with all the sunshine pouring down that he wanted to let the energy pour through him instead of holding it inside.

This must be how his brother Gideon felt while pulling lightning, all that hot power searing through his muscles, his veins. They had this in common, the connection with raw power. All the members of the far-flung Raintree clan had some power, some heightened ability, but only members of the royal family could channel and control the earth's natural energies.

Dante wasn't just of the royal family, he was the Dranir, the leader of the entire clan. "Dranir" was synonymous with king, but the position he held wasn't ceremonial, it was one of sheer power. He was the oldest son of the previous Dranir, but he would have been passed over for the position if he hadn't also inherited the power to hold it.

Behind him came Al's distinctive knock on the door. The outer office was empty, Dante's secretary having gone home hours before. "Come in," he called, not turning from his view of the sunset.

The door opened, and Al said, "Mr. Raintree, this is Lorna Clay."

Dante turned and looked at the woman, all his senses on alert. The first thing he noticed was the vibrant color of her hair, a rich, dark red that encompassed a multitude of shades from copper to burgundy. The warm amber light danced along the iridescent strands, and he felt a hard tug of sheer lust in his gut. Looking at her hair was almost like looking at fire, and he had the same reaction.

The second thing he noticed was that she was spitting mad.

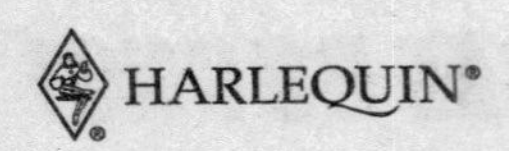

INTRIGUE®

COMING NEXT MONTH

#987 COWBOY SANCTUARY by Elle James
Bodyguards Unlimited, Denver, CO (Book 3 of 6)
A dying man's word leads bodyguard Cameron Morgan back to his family's ranch—and face-to-face with Jennie Ward. But his high school sweetheart is the daughter of a rival rancher, leading to old wounds being reopened as a feud is reignited.

#988 COUNCIL OF FIRE by Aimée Thurlo
Circle of Warriors
Hunter Blueeyes is one of the Circle of Warriors, an elite group of Navajo. Chosen to protect Lisa Garza, they embark on a quest to restore the tribe's lost honor, fraught with peril and consuming love.

#989 HOSTAGE SITUATION by Debra Webb
Colby Agency: The Equalizers (Book 2 of 3)
In her new career with the Equalizers, Renee Vaughn is to use Paul Reyes to lure a drug lord out of hiding. But when the tables are turned, the emotions they can't conceal may get them killed.

#990 UNDERCOVER DADDY by Delores Fossen
Five-Alarm Babies
Elaina McLemore was living a quiet life in Texas with her adopted son until Luke Buchanan showed up, claiming he was her long-lost husband. Convincing all of Crystal Creek—and a killer—was easy compared to not acting on their impulses.

#991 IRONCLAD COVER by Dana Marton
Mission: Redemption (Book 2 of 4)
It was Brant Law's last case as an FBI agent, and Anita Caballo was going to help him take down an arms dealer. Going undercover meant no more lies—at least, not to each other.

#992 JUROR NO. 7 by Mallory Kane
Targeted by the mob, Lily Raines's only hope is rugged enforcer Jake Brand. But after rescuing her from a botched hit, Jake's struggles to keep from being exposed as an undercover cop are forever linked with Lily's escape from certain death.

www.eHarlequin.com

HICNM0407